Cui Bono

Reed Stirling

Print ISBNs
Amazon print 9780228638698
Ingram Spark 9780228638704
Barnes & Noble 9780228638711
BWL Print 9780228638728

[BWL Publishing logo with business url]

Copyright 2026 by J. C. McKenna
Editor Nancy M. Bell
Cover artist Michelle Lee

Dedication

For Mike and Nancy Downes

Acknowledgements

"Whom the gods would destroy, they first make mad."

— ancient proverb

"All concerns of men go wrong when they wish to cure evil with evil."

— Sophocles

"Oh, good Apollo, for the final effort, make me such a vessel of your genius, as you demand for the gift of your beloved laurel."

—Dante, the *Divine Comedy*

BWL Publishing acknowledges the Government of Canada and the Canada Book Fund for its financial support.

Funded by the Government of Canada | Canada

[Government of Canada Logo]

BWL Publishing acknowledges the Province of Alberta for their ongoing support through the Alberta Publishers Cultural Industry Operating Grant.

Alberta Government

[Government of Alberta logo]

Table of Contents

[Certified Canadian Publisher Badge]

Chapter 1
Bistro Massimo

Exiting Washington Square where she had taken a casual, afternoon stroll, Lucy Hunter crossed over to Sixth Avenue and headed down towards Carmine Street. Jetlag was never really a problem for her, so getting out and about was what she enjoyed most when visiting foreign cities. It was a time-honoured scheme she developed for "easing into location" as she put it to her director at Reporters Without Borders earlier in her career. Greenwich Village rated high on locations she loved to ease into.

The weather this day was agreeable enough: warm and humid and a little close. An occasional rumble of thunder in the distance inspired Lucy to conceive of an impetuous Zeus stomping around angrily in the greenroom of the sultry afternoon, so very impatient to assert his immortal dominance. Lucy snickered at the inanity of her passing thought. She convinced herself there was no real chance of rain despite the occasional cloud of ominous grey passing overhead; no likelihood of a cloudburst threatening to dampen her expectations. Previously, under somewhat similar circumstances where reading the signs came into play, she had been drenched in a downpour, dark clouds ponderous in the sky and thunder echoing overhead in the brick and mortar canyons of the village precincts.

She'd paused for a brief moment across from number 3 Washington Square North, where a favourite painter of hers had lived most of his life, to indulge herself in a little reverie with respect to the urban experience he projected on his many canvases. The former residence of Edward Hopper was now attached to the School of Arts and Sciences at NYU. This go around, she would definitely get to the museum exhibiting his works. She would dress up for the occasion and make time on the morning of the last day.

On an earlier assignment to New York, Lucy discovered Bistro Massimo, which was within manageable distance from her park-side hotel and decided it was the perfect spot to enjoy a little downtime after the walkabout. She sat at a table in the canopied street patio, hooked her daypack over the back of a chair, and ordered a Yemeni latte from the young waiter who immediately attended to her. Shades of the Mediterranean, Lucy reflected in an up frame of mind, colourful awnings, big picture windows, potted plants, the aromas of Greek food and other delectables, even eavesdropping on a trio of students two tables away debating the nature of fate. Noise from passing traffic was muffled, fumes restricted. All was good. She allowed a memory of the fragrant spike-headed hyacinth attracting the neighbour bees to cap off the feeling of well-being. When done at the Bistro Massimo, she planned to saunter along Bleecker Street for a few blocks, cut up to enjoy the ambiance of active neighbourhoods, and circle back to the hotel. Habitual in such meandering around the village was identifying Hopperesque chiaroscuro geometry high up on building walls: seeing light emerge out of shadow filled her with a sense of balance, of studied composure. Emails and replies would obviously have to wait.

Lucy tuned in when one of the students speculated that it was possible for a murderous criminal to hide in plain sight and victimize you. A twist of fate, right? Another of the students added that said murderer could operate in the shadows beyond your ability to speculate and victimize you just as easily. The function of fate as well. Right? Amused by what she was hearing, Lucy wanted to pose the debaters some questions. Who can know all the facts? In the final analysis, who's to judge? And who will judge the judge? She resisted the temptation to do so when the waiter arrived with her coffee. He retreated quickly.

From the bench at an adjacent table she picked up a discarded copy of *The Village Vine*, a neighbourhood newspaper with which she was already familiar. She flipped through the pages perusing articles of interest, her mind wandering from the content she found there to the theme of the conference she would be attending the next day. Local politics, national politics, *plus ça change*. And same on the front pages of the larger dailies with the toothy grins and smiling faces of familiar politicians and high-profile personalities– amicable, duplicitous, and cheeky, no matter the stripe or the cut of the suit. Pock faced punditry forever offering a variety of truths for public consumption. If all politics are local, as it had been said, does it follow that all local politics are personal? Must be so, Lucy reasoned, allowing her eyes to scan quickly a number of advertisements on the last few pages of the paper, from promotions for assorted products to announcements for social and cultural events. A fascinating array of possibilities, she mused, wishing she had more time in the village to indulge any number of whimsical pursuits whatever they might turn out to be. She had to decide, once her assignment was seen to, between an evening at the comedy club on Bleeker Street or possibly attending a Seamstress Quick concert that the ad in *The Village Vine* was promoting. Decisions. Always decisions.

Lucy's head shot back in a kind of reflex action. Isla Troyes! The name popped right out of the colourful, half-page oblong that contained it and swiftly burrowed into Lucy's mind with a force intense enough to register the fiercest of emotional reactions. Only once had she experienced such a mental jolt: the time she'd received a written death threat from sources unknown when she published a revealing article about Russian oligarchs on the move in London.

Attached to Islà Troyes' name was the title of a book, *Furious Truths: A Memoir in Verse*.

A flood of recollections swept along the channels of Lucy's memory, kaleidoscopic in effect and totally beyond her ability to order sequentially, among which, Isla Troyes' ear-piercing scream that echoed throughout the lower deck of the *Iphigenia*, and looming large, the look of terror on her face when rushing out of her mother's berth.

"Lady Kat now Lady Cadaver" echoed like a dark refrain from a murder mystery turned inside out to avoid being labelled noir. Lucy now wondered if she'd actually said that about the demise of Kat Steele or were they the words of another observer? No, her words. And before that disturbing event, Conrad Steele's floating body under the stern of the *Iphigenia*, the obscenity of which invited the cynical "Fitting access to the banks of the Styx."

Lucy shook her head, attempting by that action to take conscious control of her jumbled recollections. She felt bemused by what her reaction was to the sudden recognition of a name from out of the past. In figurative terms, the name Isla Troyes functioned like an invocation conjuring up assorted images in an instantaneous montage all linked to two murders in a family where constant discontent coloured what otherwise should have passed as good mannered exchanges in an agreeable social setting. "Hyphenated losers" was what another *Iphigenia* guest with a penchant for droll observations called the Steele cohort with its manifestly obvious love-hate behaviours.

A gust of wind at this moment caused the awning over the Bistro Massimo terrasse to bulge and flutter. Dust particles danced in the air. Lucy covered her cup of coffee with a deft movement of her right hand. She looked about. Plants in the planters swished. She caught an intoxicating waft of the hyacinths leaning their deep purple forms outward toward the horizontal. The tinkle of a nearby windchime sounded like notes plucked from a lyre, then quiet. The students grew momentarily silent when thunder rumbled in the distance importuning them in their discussion of fate. Pathetic fallacy, Lucy figured. No, she was just overreaching again.

She grew aware of a kind of tension stretching between the dire events that occurred on the last days of her week's excursion through the Lowlands and her frenzied memory of them. As the coil of recollection unraveled, Lucy determined that the reporter's temptation was to claim for an overheard comment more than was warranted and attribute far too much significance to it in the name of recovered truth. Nonetheless, vivid impressions continued to intensify the muddle that resulted from seeing Isla Troyes' name before her in stark red print — the family hostilities, the tears and the contorted faces, the inscrutable and sultry Alexsis Troyes, all connected to the discovery of Conrad Steele's corpse one morning and Kat Steele's the morning after. Kat's death, a suicide, as had been officially determined? Possibly not. Murder, then? Lucy could not help speculating again— a second murder, less spectacular than the first, but a murder nonetheless.

Would all this serve as material in Isla Troye's *Furious Truths*? How could it not?

And Forest Troyes, the disenfranchised brother, what ever became of him?

Lucy sipped more of her latte, determined not to let this unanticipated incursion of perplexing recollections interfere with her peaceful enjoyment of the city and the village within it she loved so much. And she would continue with preparation for the conference she was to report on in as relaxed a way as possible, as was her wont. She could not, however, ignore the surprising reaction that seeing Isla Troye's name incited. She definitely could not ignore the fetching notice in *The Village Vine* which she returned to with increased curiosity.

A faint flowery abstract provided the backdrop to the text. "Join us in an intimate and comfortably accommodating venue where award-winning poet and novelist Beatrice Beaumont will read from *Reflections*, her latest collection inspired by her latest travels. Also participating in the event is Isla Troyes, who will read from *Furious Truths: A Memoir in Verse.*

The date, the time, and the place were posted in modest but effective script: Tuesday July 23, 7 PM; 4TO Books on West 10th at Waverly. Host: Mrs. Sandra Belle.

Lucy slid the newspaper along the table and then consulted her phone to Google the exact location of the bookstore but when the young waiter returned and began his job of bussing, she focused her attention on him. He looked very competent in his tailored dark trousers and white shirt with rolled-up sleeves. She placed her phone on the table and slid it into a position exactly between the pepper and the salt.

"Bert, is it, according to your name tag? Short for Umberto, yeah?"

"Yes, ma'am, Bert, short for Umberto."

"That is a proper name."

"Like Umberto Eco, the writer and philosopher. He's big in semiotics."

"Semiotics?"

"How to read signs and symbols. You know, like in foreshadowing."

"I knew that."

"I'm sure you did, ma'am."

It seemed to Lucy that Bert, short for Umberto, would tower over her if she were to stand up and actually take the measure of him. He had bright, animated eyes, a swarthy complexion, and a crown of dark curly hair. What she immediately found attractive in his businesslike efficiency was that he looked her straight in the eye. The young man wasn't shy in the least.

"Tell me, Bert, the time it takes to get to Tenth Street? From Washington Square, say? Along Waverly."

"One minute by bike. Five minutes at a good clip if you're walking. Ten if you dawdle. You don't strike me as a dawdler."

"True. So, a five minute walk, more or less. Cheers, mate."

"No problem."

"The point is, Bert," Lucy proceeded to explain, taken with the alacrity she detected in him and wanting to engage him further, "I'm planning to attend an evening poetry reading at 4TO Books but I'll likely be running late."

"Running, ma'am? You mentioned walking."

"I see you have a playful spirit, Bert. A student, are you?"

Bert laid his tray down at the end of the adjacent table. "Yes, ma'am," he answered. "At NYU, studying Polisci. Summer session started this morning. Theories of Democracy, July 24 to August 15."

"That's brilliant. Political Science, then."

"That's right, ma'am."

"You Americans do acronyms so well, yeah? Polisci. It's brilliant."

"Yes, ma'am. We live in a maze of acronyms and abbreviations. Like with 4TO. The book store. It's short for Quarto, ma'am."

"Yes, of course. I was cognizant of that."

"I'm sure you were, ma'am."

"Forget the ma'am bit, yeah? I'm Lucy. Call me Lucy, short for Lucille."

"Will do, Lucy. I see you're from the UK. England, judging by the Union Jack on the flap of your backpack. I also noted the accent."

"Righto, Bert," Lucy said and then smiled.

Bert returned the smile. It appeared as though he were enjoying the exchanges with this perky little woman from across the pond. She had a pretty face with rosy cheeks and alert brown eyes that radiated intelligence. Had he been queried about her schoolmarmish appearance, he might have answered that her wire rim glasses suited her well, added a touch of the eccentric to her agreeable personality, and that she came across as quick-witted as his favourite prof or his first quaff of grappa.

"We Brits have our own way of expressing things. Pavement versus sidewalk, yeah? Loo for toilet. Some of us are very lazy about pronouncing r's. We elide, as in omit the sound of. So 'far' becomes 'fah' and so on. Clipped vowels, like. Depends on where you come from. I've been called campy, not in what I say, but in how I say it."

"I read you, Lucy."

"I'm here on assignment for the Bureau of Investigative Reporting," Lucy went on to explain. "London-based, so I am. This assignment will involve less digging out the facts than is usual. Tomorrow I'll be attending a conference on autocracy right here at the NYU School of Law."

"Autocracy here at the NYU School of Law, ma'am? I wasn't aware..."

"Well played! Wit served on a polished aluminum tray, yeah?

"I blush with embarrassment."

"Please understand, Bert, that my written prose is usually more succinct than my spoken word."

"I'm sure it is, Lucy."

"Succinct but pedestrian in my fact-based approach to drawing conclusions. When inspired, I can think poetically or metaphorically, and come up with a clever image or express a concept that startles me in my most down-to-earth frame of mind."

"Right on. How will you approach Challenging Autocracy in America?"

"Directly. Try to separate fact from fantasy in writing up my report. I have to judge the value and efficacy of what is proposed. And just who is saying what."

"So you're judgemental."

"That word has various connotations, Bert. I'm sure you agree. Better to say I exercise judgement based on observation and research and fact finding and dogged pursuit of the truth."

"Ever been challenged for what you write?"

"Occasionally. If uncertain, I tend not to publish. I've been called beady-eyed and overly critical. More than once."

"Things don't always add up perfectly, do they? Sometimes what is true lies far from what is perceived as true. Appearances can be deceiving, as they say. The burden of proof and all that."

"Very perceptive, Bert."

"Just common sense, really. You know, I plan to attend that conference tomorrow."

"Super. An avid student of politics. As you probably know, then, the list of attendees and speakers is impressive. Scholars, political commentators, reporters, everyday people, and we'll be among them."

"Yes, ma'am. Lucy. And pundits. I've a scholarly interest in the threat posed by the conservative Roadmap 2.0 and its likely effects on education. At times I'm completely overwhelmed by the staggering stupidity and ignorance of the man who is foremost among its advocates. No words suffice."

"Indeed. Very clever of you. Very involved. The countermeasures to be discussed will likely form the thrust of my report."

"Right on."

"Unfortunately, the hour dedicated to that kind of response to the established autocratic threat conflicts with the time posted for the poetry reading I mentioned."

"So you will have to hustle, Lucy."

"Indeed I will," Lucy said and grimaced.

"You wear sensible walking shoes, Lucy. No sweat."

Lucy imagined Bert silently amused by the image of her leaving the conference in a dither and hopping it along Beverly Street in her sensible shoes. Regardless, she was set on hearing Isla Troyes read. As Bert moved over to the table he intended to clear, she explained her situation further. "The conference is a one-day affair, so I'll have a couple of discretionary days afterwards. These get-aways with time off provide relief from the usual grind."

"Have you been to New York before?"

"Several times. The last visit had me report on a symposium dealing with universal justice, international law, and the role of *lex talionis*"

"*Lex talionis*," Bert said, aligning his tray just so on the table and pulling back a step.

"Justice in the form of revenge."

"Eye for an eye. Tooth for a tooth. And a dolla for a dolla even if it's dirty money and a bloodied baseball bat serves as the agent of exchange."

"Quite. Violent tit for tat. Or one's promised pound of flesh, as it were. Sometimes it's just a matter of personal vendetta that goes beyond Tennyson's *nature red in tooth and claw*. The poet, yeah?"

Bert inclined his head to the side in acknowledgement. Looking over to the entrance to the bistro, he made to pick up his tray and get down to business. Before doing so, he asked, "Can I bring you anything else, Lucy?"

"Not at the moment, but thank you, Bert."

"No problem."

Lucy carried on talking, elaborating on the theme of personal vendetta. "It exemplifies the willfulness of an autocrat to exact revenge against an individual perceived as opposition or enemy."

Lucy quickly dismissed the pop-up image of Conrad Steele holding court at the family table on the *Iphigenia* and admonishing those he found disagreeable, Alexsis in particular, and his son Boyd Alexander right behind her.

"Or critic," Bert added.

"And then add into the equation the claim of having the right, due to his high position, to take any woman he wants, young or old, with or without her consent, as in the days of the ascendent French aristocracy, their *droits des seigneurs*."

"There's a lot of that going around these days," Bert said, sneering slightly. "I suppose in your work you do have to exercise judgement."

"Absolutely. Making the right decision about revealing corruption in high places and whatnot has its downside even if culprits get arrested and offenders get tried in courts of law. Reprisals, yeah?"

"Yeah, I understand how that can work against you, the reporter."

When the trio of students leave, they wave their good-byes and Bert responds. Lucy explains how she overheard them discussing Fate.

"They're here all the time. Sometimes it's football, sometimes it's music and literature, sometimes it's the overreach of the cops."

"It's a popular spot here for students, no doubt. Regarding the conference, Bert, at 5:30 there's a scheduled break for drinks. Cocktails and conversations, part of the overall agenda. Perhaps you'll be able to bring me a cordial from the bar at that time. We'll be able to compare notes. Your insights I could use in my report— you know, from the point of view of American youth."

"Or back here at Bistro Massimo. I'm a full-time student with a part-time job. There are many in a similar situation. We take the shifts we're given. *My* agenda has me here at six tomorrow evening."

"So you, too, will have to hustle. Pity."

Bert nodded oddly — a gesture of regret coupled with appreciation for Lucy's return serve. She smiled up at him indulgently.

Bert explained: "My present course, Theories of Democracy, immerses me in some pretty extensive reading. Plato and the usual suspects, including Payne, Jefferson, and Madison. H. L. Mencken provides me with a sideline view of American society."

"Heavy indeed, Bert."

"Going to Chicago, Lucy?" Bert asked off the cuff, seemingly willing to extend the conversation despite the insistence of the messy table. "For the Democratic convention?"

"Not assigned there. Not yet anyway."

"The Paris Olympics?"

"Not so far."

A young woman sauntered by pushing a stroller and sang out, "Be Bop a Doula, she's my baby now, my baby now."

"Get outta hea," Bert said in mock petulance. He threw his hands out in a *what's all this* kind of gesture and then laughed delightedly. He turned to Lucy and explained. "Our neighbour, Gina Vincente. Her first child. Very happy. Unusual delivery."

"Brilliant," Lucy commented, watching as the young woman called Gina Vincente proceeded past the bistro.

"She used to serve tables here too," Bert said, piling plates on his tray just so. "Now, not so much."

"Quite."

"Talking of autocracy and the theatre of cruelty where its oppressive powers are exercised," Bert said, interrupting the cleaning-up, "the Vincentes suffered in the old country during Mussolini's scourge. Family members were 'disappeared' during the night, believed murdered. Tribal feuding was what Fascist officials offered as an explanation. Possible but extremely doubtful according to table talk I'd hear as a kid when being babysat next door."

"There it is again. *Lex talionis*, even as used by the totalitarian state in its deception and cover-up. Typical of dictatorship. Typical of autocracy."

Lucy was enjoying the give and take with this bright young student and believed that he was enjoying it as well. After all, they had a common interest and would be attending the same conference. She realized, however, that despite her inquisitive but friendly ways, she was distracting him from his duties.

"Thank you, Bert," she said pleasantly, acknowledging his imminent withdrawal inside by waving her hand. "It's been a pleasure conversing with you. Good luck with your studies. See you tomorrow, yeah?"

"A good bet, that. Know what, Lucy, I like the effect of your earrings. Like a little silver chain."

Lucy laughed at the compliment. Given the academic downgrading of universities in the UK intending to placate society's wounded, she wondered if the same applied here in America. Bert, however, appeared to exemplify the essential qualities of character and intellect that merited her approval. Not only that, his sense of timing was impeccable. She waved him away.

Chapter 2
The Village Vine

When Bert finished clearing the table and headed into the bistro, his tray in hand laden with cups and plates and cutlery, Lucy picked up her phone again with the intention of going online to research Isla Troyes' reading engagement. Under "4TO Books" she sussed out significant additional information about the event beyond the who, what, where and when that *The Village Vine* had given her. Date and time were confirmed. Press kits were provided on the site for both poets. Book covers. Bios. Photos. All relevant Links. Lucy felt inundated with material but she liked the sensation that always came over her when needing to delve into matters, when "fishing for facts," as she called it.

Furious Truths: A Memoir in Verse. The title of the book struck Lucy initially as somewhat ambivalent; it bespoke considerable intellectual ambition on Isla's part. Interestingly, the cover featured Erato, the mythological Greek muse of poetry. Erato, yes, certainly, Lucy recognized her well enough, but she was not depicted with myrtle and roses, playing the lyre. Nor was she surrounded by a host of Cupid-like putti fussing about as was often the case when artists followed classical tradition. Her wings and her lyre, half-delineated details in the representation, Lucy considered no more than necessary afterthoughts; they were in the frame but were merely suggestive of Erato's abilities rather than central to defining her role as source of poetic and musical inspiration for mortals. Erato's left hand rested upon the edge of the lyre: "Enough of that plucking for now," Lucy heard herself declare on behalf of the muse in an interpretation of the restrained gesture, "there's something over there more worthy of my attention." That was a logical enough extrapolation Lucy decided as she continued to evaluate the cover and how Erato was presented with her other hand, fingers folded in upon themselves, supporting her angled, laurel-crowned head. The index finger pointed subtly to her temple while her eyes seemed to be focused on some abstract form outside the space of the composition. This was the muse Erato arrested in a pose of pure contemplation.

The cover left Lucy with the impression, if a book can ever be judged by its cover, that the content of the volume would likely tend to be less lyrical in its revelation of "furious truths" and more pensive, more analytical, more introspective. Erato definitely looked bemused.

The cover for Beatrice Beaumont's *Reflections* was comprised of a collage of medieval motifs. The title was printed in banquet script across the top with her name in more modest print at the bottom. It was similar to how Isla's cover looked, only the title was considerably larger and more banner-like.

Isla's bio, simple and direct, included mention of the journals and poetry magazines that had accepted her work. She was described as being "very up" about having her first volume of poetry published. It had been a struggle. Blurb information was more suggestive of source material and inspiration than specific in its detail regarding origins. Lucy wondered about the other members of the Troyes family that had burst upon her consciousness so insistently when she first read Isla's name in *The Village Vine* announcement. What might their influence have been on Isla, what "furious truths" might they have imposed on her in the self-revelation her verse purported to deliver? The bio concluded with confirming that Isla Troyes was a student in the NYU creative writing program and was lucky and delighted to call Greenwich Village home.

Beatrice Beaumont's bio, on the other hand, was more extensive; it included information on the countries she had travelled to and provided an extensive bibliography of publications that appeared under her name, from chapbooks to travel articles. It mentioned several poetry prizes she had won. Beatrice Beaumont, aka L. L. Lacey, was also a writer of cozy mysteries that featured the clever, smalltown sleuth called Olivia St. Jude. Lucy remembered reading one of the Lacey's novels on a vacation to Corfu.

The book blurb for Beaumont's *Reflections* was detailed, replete with a variety of reviews, all positive, as in, for instance, "a masterful manifestation of the probing spirit." Lucy wondered if the same claim might be made of Isla's poetic endeavours. Lucy Hunter, investigative reporter in a rush, definitely intended to find out.

Photos: among which, shots of both poets holding their books.

Beatrice Beaumont appeared to like the camera: she was smiling benevolently and looked as though she had deliberately decked herself out for the photo shoot in efforts to present an accurate picture of who she could be, externally, at least: colourful headband, large silver loops at her ears, bangles on her arms, rings galore, and so much more, all wrapped up in a whimsical print dress. A quintessential portrait of boho chic.

Isla Troyes came across as more reserved, demure, and definitely less flamboyant than what her counterpart presented to her potential readers and to the world at large. Lucy fiddled with her string of earrings that the waiter Bert so admired as she studied Isla's photo. She remembered Isla Troyes as plain in her appearance and making little attempt to change that appearance, so unlike her cousin Candace who had been her constant companion when Lucy met and talked with them on the boat and bike excursion through the Lowlands. Isla had certainly been less animated than her more vocal sister Alexsis, except for when she discovered her mother lying stiff and immobile that last morning. Lucy wondered if maybe she were reading too much into the face in the photograph before her, overlaying impressions she had about people and events that occurred on the *Iphigenia* two and a half years previously. Perhaps so, but she remembered that Isla Troyes was patient and accepting but not without a stiffer side, bolstered by a streak of self-assertiveness, that only became apparent in the Bruges hotel after the fact when the fallout dust from the two deaths was still floating about and causing great uncertainty. Isla had her opinions, certainly, and voiced them when the need arose. She was living proof, as far as Lucy was concerned, that one's reservation about offering an opinion did not equate to not having one at all. Isla Troyes' reticence might simply have disguised her more authentic self, a self that a couple of years later definitely did not in any way project the image of boho chic.

On a previous visit to New York City and the village, Lucy had attended a reading at The Bookstore located on East Twelfth street. She bought a signed copy of the novel being promoted, a whodunit set in Greece by a relatively obscure writer. Tomorrow would be different. Knowing author Isla Troyes was one thing. Being very familiar at one time with the turn of events on the *Iphigenia* that affected Isla Troyes and her family would have a great deal more relevance for an interested listener such as Lucy Hunter intended to be. That was another thing, indeed. The Troyes story, which so intrigued her even as she worked on the assignment in Paris that immediately followed her week on the *Iphigenia,* somehow got lost in subsequent news cycles. She postulated plausible explanations without factual certainty and moved on. Total fabrication, Lucy reminded herself, could result in any effort to animate memory when significant events from past experiences could hide among the vagaries of time itself. Absolute in her wanting to know, she looked forward to being present for the readings at 4TO Books with a great deal of anticipation.

Chapter 3
Happy Families

The Waverly Hotel, located on the edge of Washington Square, suited Lucy in every way. Her account there had originally been set up by Reporters Without Borders, an arrangement that the Bureau of Investigative Reporting retained on her behalf. The long-established hotel on Waverly Place had once been described to Lucy as boutique, genteel and yet urbane. Lovely, absolutely perfect. Lucy loved the Art Deco touches. The antique, rolltop desk was brilliant. The mirror by the entrance never lied to her about what she saw reflected there as she left in a hurry or retired in slow motion. The small, comfortable, well-appointed rooms suited her purposes to a T when she was writing up her reports and not out taking in local Village sites by day or being entertained in the evening at any of the many Bleeker Street attractions. Adjacent to the hotel was the Four Square Restaurant, which served excellent fare, and a block away was the convenient West Fourth Street-Washington Square Station.

Preparation for the conference on Challenging Autocracy in America was basic, formulaic, virtually rote in its particulars. What Lucy Hunter had in mind beyond that would likely take considerable time so she ordered a meal by phone from the Four Square Restaurant, the nearest take-away service available she could find. Wanting something fast, she ordered fast food, pastrami on rye, a New York sandwich she always found appetizing.

"Double the pickles, yeah?" she shouted into the phone.

By the time the pastrami sandwich was delivered, Lucy had jotted down in her notebook a number of points, establishing a vague sequence based on what she remembered from her own conversations with members of the Conrad Steele group like Isla Troyes and Alexsis Troyes and from what other guests on the *Iphigenia* had communicated to her, most notably Geoff Cantor and Frank Veridis. Initial impetus for Lucy's reports and political commentaries always took the form of handwritten points which she expanded and then transcribed into a computer file and worked diligently into a polished, publishable piece. In terms of present considerations, namely the Troyes family intrigue, she ordered her jottings into headings numbered One, Two, Three, and Four.

She paid and tipped the delivery boy and immediately took a bite of her pastrami sandwich and then a swing from the bottle of spring water she'd also ordered. She relished her pickles and chomped down on each of them with increasing delight as she reviewed the four major rubrics (she had a fondness for the term) that would align in logical sequence the narrative she hoped to pull together. After finishing off her sandwich and swallowing every last drop of tangy succulence from the last of her pickles, she developed a craving for pudding, chocolate she imagined. She wrapped her hands around her head and began wondering and supposing. Isla Troyes' *Furious Truths: A Memoir in Verse* functioned like a catalyst to *temps perdu*.

One: Jennifer Troyes, daughter of Victor and Kat Troyes, was abducted and held for ransom, but due to failed paternal manipulation she was lost to the family. This apparently resulted in Kat's enduring rancour.

Two: Victor Troyes was murdered in a hit and run operation; the death of his mistress Cassandra Fortune followed.

Three: Conrad Steele married the widow Kat and dominated the remaining Troyes children, Forrest, Alexsis, and Isla. They grew suspicious and resentful of the new arrangement. Forrest was ostracised and remained isolated from the family well into his twenties. Forrest Troyes remained a figure of mystery.

Four: On the recent boat and bike excursion through the Lowlands on the *Iphigenia*, Conrad Steele was murdered. Kat's death, termed a suicide, followed.

As she fantasized about chocolate pudding, Lucy asked herself a number of questions, the most obvious being what constituted plausible motivation in all three episodes involving the Troyes Family where members of that family were victims of murder, including in all likelihood the abducted Jennifer? She knew that there was so much more to uncover about how one thing led to another, how, as Shakespeare, following the pattern established by classical Greek dramatists, emphasized in dramatic detail the certainty that blood will have blood. She knew her four point-form findings were decidedly skeletal, no more than provisional. Instinctively, she understood the absolute need to dig deeper. She was determined to bundle into a more comprehensive and cohesive narrative the barrage of human images from earlier in the day and add factual content into all that she recalled. She needed to understand the significance of Conrad Steele's severed finger, the missing ring, sundry comments, and, weirdly, echoes of "Mack the Knife" from the karaoke celebrations the crew organized on the penultimate night of the *Iphigenia* adventure. How to interpret such a weird assortment of factors? The cork top of the quirky jug, no more than a bit of circumstantial detail or symbolic of meaningful purpose? She understood the need to go back farther than that week on the barge and pull out the thematic link that made sense of it all. Like in the discussion the students at the bistro were having, she wondered if a murderer could hide in plain sight?

Finding fact was the convention Lucy Hunter most relied on in reaching conclusions in the many official reports she had been required to produce for Reporters Without Borders and these days for the Bureau of Investigative Reporting. Speculation had its place and often led to uncovering evidence that had a bearing on a theme being developed, a social issue, for instance, one requiring immediate redress. On her laptop she had innumerable files reflective of all her endeavours as an investigative reporter. The laptop was an organ of research as well as a repository of treasured information. Reviewing old stories, of disaster or otherwise, was like looking in the rearview mirror to monitor the recent past or like consulting the index of a technical manual or, better yet, like fingering through a book on espionage for items of interest such as the methods employed in the elimination of perceived enemies, political assassinations foremost in the annals of not only foreign but also domestic intrigue.

Memories could fracture and fragment, she reminded herself as she got up and walked around the room. She approached the window that in the light of day gave onto Beverly but at this point in the late evening she saw only her own reflection, that of a frizzy, grey-haired, middle aged woman frowning in silver laced dismay. Okay, thirtyish. Misremembering could conflate two or more observations, she reasoned, the particulars of an embarrassing scene combined with a stern admonition, for example, and deliver an absolute misrepresentation of what actually took place. Moreover, misremembering could inflate the import of no more than a fatuous impression. Gossip, innuendo, and insinuation could slant assessment of an overheard conversation and lead to something false being taken for truc. Bcrt at the Bistro Massimo had been correct in reminding her of the error in assuming too much in the service of speculation or mere suspicion. His common sense understanding of ambiguous issues echoed. How had he put it? Sometimes what is true lies far from what is perceived as true. Appearances betray fact.

The laptop contained files Lucy could rely on because she knew them to be absolutely authentic; as to their absolute truth, it would be difficult to determine absolutely. Info on the Troyes Family gathered previously, quickly available or buried in confusion or lost forever in an

Orwellian memory hole. Whatever, she was determined to find that info. Drawing on all her resources, she hoped to align events in a logical sequence that best served the facts and that got to the very heart of the matter.

Bearing down, Lucy entertained this thought: Isla may be the poet, and may have been one when she met her on the *Iphigenia,* but Alexsis was, and may still continue to be, the communicator. In addition to conversing with the two sisters in the aftermath of what all onboard understood to be tragic but disturbingly mysterious at the same time, it was Alexsis who provided Lucy with two very thorough personal accounts of how Troyes Family discord and dysfunction resulted in large regrets. And by extension, how Steele Family discord and dysfunction resulted in the two deaths that all the guests on the *Iphigenia* puzzled over, Lucy, the investigative reporter, not the least among them. She would dig out and review her own online probing of news articles related to Troyes Family history that the sisters hinted at and fuse them into the tentative conclusions about *what* really happened on the *Iphigenia* and *why* it happened the way it did. She'd come to believe back then that the acrimony witnessed in the Conrad Steele group started a long time ago, long before the dissolution of Kat and Victor's marriage, ages ago, in fact. The observant Geoff Canter, whom she met by chance in Paris after departing the *Iphigenia,* had been party to her speculations and agreed in part with what they implied. Was his agreement relevant? An irrelevant question, more rhetorical than purposeful.

Back then, Lucy had been compelled to get beyond material gleaned from family members met on the *Iphigenia*, compelled to delve into all sources available on the internet, all the serviceable dot com sites, even drawing on the files in the archives of Reporters Without Borders, ditto for The Bureau of Investigative Journalism. Thus, a great deal of digging— dates, newspaper articles (ingeniously bypassing paywalls), media reports, police statements, podcasts, the whole gamut, even archived interviews with Victor Troyes himself.

Before hitting the pillow, Lucy had expanded her four points considerably. Extrapolations were as accurate as she could determine given the limitations of her recovered sources.

One: Isla and Alexsis were the daughters of Victor and Kat Troyes, as was Jennifer, who was the eldest of four children. Forrest Troyes was their son. In sorting through the material on hand, Lucy uncovered what Alexsis conveyed in her efforts to inform Lucy of the web of shifting allegiances that she believed was the basis for the serious rift that opened between her mother and her father. Existing conflict intensified with the abduction of Jennifer Troyes when she was twenty and a sophomore at university. Her loss continued to be the source of sadness, regret, and contention; the blame game broke out with vehemence and intensified over time to the dismay of the younger children.

A ransom demand for millions ensued after Jennifer was nabbed at night while returning to her dorm from the library. Rather than follow procedures sanctioned by the FBI, Victor Troyes opted to have his barrister Calvin Kinlaw conduct negotiations with the kidnappers in a manner he himself prescribed. Kinlaw failed to achieve positive results, leaving Victor Troyes not only thwarted in his scheme to outsmart the kidnappers but also subjected to ignominious condemnation by his wife, Kat, who told him point-blank and often that he'd fucked up royally and that her beloved Jennifer was lost.

Two: According to Alexsis, Victor Troyes was taken out in a hit and run crash. His Mercedes was rammed full on by a speeding Hummer and crushed against a concrete ramp. A targeted homicide according to police authorities. Like with the Jennifer Troyes' abduction, the Victor Troyes' case was yet to be solved. A week after his remains were laid to rest, his long-standing personal secretary Cassandra Fortune was found dead in her apartment. The coroner established the cause of her death to be an overdose of heroin. However, suicide was eliminated as the cause of death.

Three: Doubt was raised in young Alexsis' mind as to how her father died and that early doubt continued to increase in volume as the years passed. She felt certain that Conrad Steele and her mother Kat had arranged for the elimination of both her father and his mistress, Cassandra Fortune. Her aggrieved brother Forrest was of the same mind. And Virgil Troyes, her uncle, had his suspicions as well. She claimed that everything just fell too perfectly into place for Conrad and Kat— the quick marriage, his assuming control of the AEP company over which her father had presided, the ensuing abuse, the loss of inheritance.

Alexsis' resentment later found eloquent expression in an essay on gaslighting which she titled *The Creation of a False Narrative*, a copy of which she eventually forwarded to Lucy. In seeking absolute control through manipulation and deceit, Conrad Steele robbed the Troyes children of the life their father had promised them, Alexsis declared categorically, denying them freedom of action, of movement, of choice. They were victims of gaslighting. Therefore their personal memories got distorted or revamped. In time, Forrest was sent away, virtually abandoned by his mother. Lies and deceit regarding his state of mind and his very existence became commonplace. Isla's passivity contrasted with Alexsis' non-compliance and her loud vocal opposition to the imperious Conrad and Kat. It was dark behaviour that Lucy and other guests on the *Iphigenia* noted and commented on while they cycled and barged through the Lowlands.

Four: Conrad Steele, assumed father-figure for the duration, was murdered in Bruges. His body was found floating beneath the stern of the *Iphigenia* by members of the crew. Lucy remembered seeing his recovered corpse lying in a heap, a lifeless impersonation of the autocratic paterfamilias he had been, and conjured up in her mind's eye the rictus of regret etched indelibly into his face. Down on the quay as close to the corpse as was permitted, Kat continued banging on the flagstones with clenched fists, calling out her husband's name between heightened cries of disbelief and curses directed at anyone who approached her. Guests were looking on from the upper deck of the *Iphigenia* like a chorus of incredulous gawkers, phone cameras ready to record. What stood out most in Lucy's recollection of the scene was Kat's near hysterical response to her husband's calamitous end. There was no consoling her.

Said one: "He's a gross embarrassment, totally lacking basic human identity."

Said another: "The lady doth protest too much, me thinks!"

"Brilliant," Lucy said to herself, almost embarrassed by such detailed recall.

By evening's end of that dreadful day, substantial incriminating evidence led to the arrest by Belgian authorities of one Dolf Van Handelaar who was charged with the murder of Conrad Steele. Kat Steele was found dead the next morning by her daughter Isla. Suicide was what police officials and the medical examiner concluded, given the evidence in the cabin and the fact that a very distraught Kat, hysterical with grief, had just lost her husband.

Lucy supposed it was logical to accept that Kat committed suicide. She cursed herself for failing to dig out of her vault of hidden computer files the extended communication received from Alexsis, the one she shared with Geoff Canter in Paris; it was full of inferences and a series of *what ifs* on Alexsis' part that never got explained satisfactorily. Lucy was also unable to pull up *The Creation of a False Narrative*, Alexsis' essay on gaslighting. At least she remembered the title.

On the verge of mental exhaustion, Lucy wrestled with some final considerations, the question of *Cui bono* being of primary interest. Who benefited, who gained? Was it all simply an extended version of the zero sum game of Happy Families? Or was it no more than some unknown entity enjoying a rather complicated and sinister last laugh?

"It's like following myself down a rabbit hole into the darkest recesses of human imagining," Lucy told herself, remonstration taking hold of her thoughts, "where fascination and horror share the same landscape."

Lucy Hunter, investigative reporter par excellence, wanted to know what induced the brain to produce images that distracted you or for that matter attracted you, that awakened you with a start, or that launched you off your puffed-up pillow into an analytical abyss where brume was ubiquitous and foggy thinking was the only medium of discourse.

"Enough!"

She called it a night, prepared for bed having taken care of perfunctory personal rituals, and hit the pillow with the hope, vague though it was, that Isla Troye's poetry revelations would... Would what? She could not determine what.

She grabbed the remote from the bedside table, turned on the small television on the wall that was angled perfectly for watching from bed, and sought the music channels that held sway beyond the range of the contentious talking heads immersed in the issues of the day like the threat of autocracy she'd have to spend hours auditing next day and then reporting on. Despite the multiplicity of channels available to her,

Lucy considered viewing options very limited and overwrought with strings of inane commercials: AI or computer generated heroes in films that appealed to adolescent male mentality where insurmountable threats to human existence got sorted by the end of the script, often with the aid of bioluminescence; or violent adult combat attractions like extreme boxing or sexy female wrestling bouts that appealed to the wanton male caught in middle life crisis. *Plus ca change—*

She was aware that what had been her primary reason for being in New York City had been upstaged by the Troyes Family saga.

"Brilliant!" she said in a self-deprecating voice, wanting no more at this juncture than to just let go.

She tuned into Chopin's Nocturne Op 9 No 1 that had just begun airing. She closed her eyes, took a deep breath, and began to drift, the knotted brow relaxing the deeper her head she sank into the pillows. She felt as though the music was already at work soothing her addled brain. She welcomed the dreamy image of Apollo, god of music and all creative inspiration, under a laurel tree playing, not his harp, but a grand piano. She may well have been smiling at this point.

Chapter 4
Roadmap 2.0

Challenging Autocracy in America opened at eleven A.M. Every chair in the extensive conference room was occupied by the time the moderator took to the microphone. He laid out the rules of the proceedings and then reviewed the schedule of events, all but the break for drinks from five-thirty to six taking the form of panel discussions at the big table. He then named, to much applause, distinguished individuals from both sides of the political spectrum who would be participating in discussions.

Lucy Hunter sat at the back of the room and drank in the atmosphere. She felt confident that necessary things would be subject to close scrutiny here and was very pleased to be present to bear witness. It was all about urgency. Waiting for the first panel to begin, she did a quick sketch of the NYU law school emblem highlighted on the podium: the symbol of justice, scales balanced, favouring neither one side nor the other. Justice— so difficult to ensure when autocracy takes hold in an otherwise free and liberal society. While doodling (a habit of hers formed over the years that evinced curiosity, expectation, and patience in equal order), Lucy experienced at this juncture several adrenal rushes that jolted her inquisitive mind. She hoped they were instances of divine afflatus, Apollo preferably, being that he was the ancient god of justice. Given her divided attention, autocracy and the Troyes Family intrigue, these impulses were not totally unexpected.

Throughout the events of the day, Lucy would take copious notes. As was usual, they were handwritten, using the shorthand she'd refined over the years: transcribed later into a computer file, they would form the content of her reports. Despite the serious nature of the theme, the mood of the conference was by and large uplifting, positive vibes evident in a united effort to understand and confront the obvious threats posed by autocracy. Where a sombre tone might have dominated discussions, and though speakers were serious in what they had to impart to the audience and to each other, they were amenable to humorous anecdotes, ironic asides, and witty repartee.

Beyond expected areas of concern voiced by the participants like voter suppression, corruption in high places including the DOJ, and fear of January 6 repeating, what Lucy found most enlightening were points delivered by those panelists on the right who had had first hand experiences of incipient totalitarianism in American political life which included a detailed description of how traditional conservative values had already been perverted. Of equal significance for Lucy's reporting was the universal anxiety about revenge politics, purges, and the bullying of professionals, all inherent in the cult of personality. One prominent speaker warned of the negative effects in the extreme messaging that was so evident in the present and the inevitable undermining of truth, where black was not black but a different kind of white. Following up on that point, another speaker, referencing Orwell, signaled the danger in allowing specific events of the recent past to slide down memory holes. These warnings gave Lucy much to pencil in.

One of the last questions posed in the public forum, which lasted from 4:30 to 5:30, concerned *Roadmap 2.0* and the censorship of fictional books like Margaret Atwood's *The Handmaid's Tale*. The question came from down near the front row. Lucy had no trouble recognizing the voice of Bert from *Bistro Massimo*. She did not find the answer to that probing question consoling in any way and was sure that Bert felt much the same. She saw him heading to the exit.

At that point in the open mike section of the program, Lucy decided to leave the assembly for a moment and reply in a text to the call that had come in from the Bureau while she had her phone on vibration mode, which was for all of the conference. She'd hoped an assignment to Paris for the Olympics was on offer, but it was not. It was a run-of-the-mill inquiry from her immediate superior regarding the eta of her report. Such promptings always left her nonplussed because she never missed a deadline, never, unless something threatening or dangerous caused an unavoidable delay, and that only happened twice. Given the five hour difference in time from London, Lucy wrote: "Get back to you at a more convenient hour, Guv." When she returned to her seat, the question of eliminating NOAA, the National Oceanic & Atmospheric Agency, led to voiced grievances regarding weather related problems including hurricanes. The half-hour reserved for drinks and less formal exchanges she welcomed with a thirst only a long draught of brew could satisfy.

Chitchat over drinks would add to Lucy's total input of detail for the day. One man pulling on a pint lamented the possible diminished effectiveness of intelligence agencies. Another had a supply of anecdotal instances to support his observations about the cult of the personality and the psychology of its followers. He put Lucy in mind of Frank Veridis from the *Iphigenia* who could hold forth in similar fashion. For the briefest of moments the image of Conrad

Steele flashed before her eyes, and naturally enough, she remembered how very domineering he had been in his behaviour at table and elsewhere on the excursion and what the Troyes girls, Alexsis in particular, recounted to support that impression. Conrad Steele, a one-time autocrat in the making. She was still miffed about being unable to pull up those two pertinent files Alexsis had sent her, the one on gas lighting and the one containing all the *what if's*. Manager supreme of folders and files, Lucy Hunter silently cursed the necessity of passwords.

A man in a turban drinking a soda expressed his worry about the possible total ascendance of white religious nationalism that Roadmap 2.0 advocated. Also joining the little circle was a woman who asked Lucy pointedly, "Do you fear for your daughters?" To this rather direct question, Lucy replied, "I have no daughters. I am not married. But if I were, and if I had daughters, and if I lived in this country, I would. I would fear for them, yeah."

The last hour of the conference centred on the ways and means to battle against autocracy, from adhering to founding principles to ensuring electoral security, integrity, and transparency. She took notes feverously, including all items brought to the fore. In Lucy's estimation, the conference ended not with a whimper but with a resounding bang.

Leaving the site of the conference just after seven P.M., Lucy rushed across Washington Square, her rucksack beating a rhythm commensurate with a sharp, quick stride. Not the first time she cursed her short legs. Beside deciding to order in food when back at the hotel, she considered how she would organize her report, which she was determined to get off the next day before noon. The notion of "obliging the Fuhrer" had come up several times in discussion; for Lucy the phrase held considerable potential as a premise. In fact, when the term was being bandied about, she considered the totalitarian regime of Hitler but also that of Mussolini and then she thought, naturally enough, of young Bert's story of brutal persecution and murder under the fascists. The conclusion of her report would develop logically from first principles and the factual support for them amassed in her notes. Lines in the pavement along Beverley marked the pace of her desire to reach her destination on Tenth Street as fast as possible.

Chapter 5
Quarto Books

Four red doors gave access to the 4To bookstore and four big windowpanes allowed for the viewing of innumerable artfully displayed titles. Upon entering, Lucy immediately understood that it was SRO and at that precise moment the place echoed with appreciation and approval. A hulk of a man with craggy face and rifled hair, sleeves of tattoos, and scent of booze about him, had barged in just ahead of her. He quickly surveyed the interior as quickly as Lucy surveyed him. He turned abruptly, seemingly in a fit of petty annoyance, and left. He was well into his middle years, Lucy judged, when he brushed her aside on rushing out. She also determined that he looked like a well-spent porn star, a stud in search of lights and an overhead mirror. A come by chance, a Johnny come lately. Perhaps not. Perhaps at this time in the evening he was hoping to get his mitts on the latest universal stamp catalogue to determine whether his latest find was worth pennies or thousands. Then again, maybe not. He just as easily could be in search of a Nietzsche compendium.

It was difficult to take in everything at once as she eased away from the foyer not wanting to draw attention to herself as a late arrival. Late arrival though she was, she was able to catch the tail-end of the applause for Beatrice Beaumont who, Lucy quickly noted, appeared to be taller than her bio pics had suggested and more moderately decked out, this version presenting in a plaid blazer and blue jeans. The poet seemed almost prim as she expressed thanks for the reception she'd received, with a special nod to Mrs. Belle whom she addressed directly and called "a superb host." She retired to the side and sat in a chair reserved for her from where, rising for a brief moment, she saw fit to add how very accommodating Mrs. Belle had been. Then she got up again and gave the woman a hug.

Had Beatrice Beaumont intentionally downplayed the boho chic for this more formal setting? Wondering about the possibility of her having done so, Lucy cast about looking for somewhere to fit in. A chair would do nicely, but apparently there were none to be had. She was still slightly winded. Puffing audibly, she continued poking gently through the assembly in one direction and then another as unobtrusively as possible.

Seating had been arranged here and there about the premises in a seemingly helter-skelter, ad hoc fashion and a double row of chairs had been set up at a reasonable distance from the podium. All occupied. Just as Lucy was uttering a silent "bullocks" to herself, a bearded young man offered her his seat in the area where books on display were dedicated to New York City, its history, and its tourist attractions. The young man had the scent of marijuana about him. Lucy thanked him without fussing. He sidled over to a pillar and lent it his support along with a couple of other stalwarts who were doing exactly the same. He reminded Lucy of a computer boffin, like her favourite back in the Bureau that she would consult with from time to time. Settling in and catching her breath, she made sure her phone was still set to vibration mode.

Silver-haired Mrs. Belle, overly luxurious in her appearance Lucy thought, took to the podium that was situated to the side of a large oak desk. "Thank you," she said, "thank you so very much Ms. Beaumont for those wonderfully delivered lines from *Reflections*. Such lasting memories, such insightful reflections of life on the road, such exotic locations, such beautiful imagery. Such daring, such verve."

Lucy judged the woman to be in her sixties and agreeable enough as a well-turned out and tuned-in host for a book signing event, except for the over-the-top breathiness of her enthusiasm and the dramatic gesturing in her stating how beautiful she thought Beaumont's imagery was and how lasting her memories of it would be, the verve and the exotic notwithstanding. The woman was gracious and officious at the same time, ingratiating and grating both. As to the books she was holding up in praise, Lucy wondered if she had read anything in them, or about them, beyond the back cover blurbs.

Decidedly settled in with her rucksack secured on the backpack of her chair, Lucy let her focus drift away momentarily from the podium and the effusive voice of Mrs. Belle. She scanned the room, taking in at a glance attendees in her immediate vicinity. These included a gaggle of senior ladies, two of them wearing natty hats that could do nothing but distract; a contingent of enthusiastic students in startling violet t-shirts; and a scattering of tufted bald pates, collared with pendular grey ponytails. Among the many standees that lined the perimeter of the interior was a couple of professorial types in mandatory tweed jackets and between them a teenager whose head was lost in a bowler hat. A clutch of giddy teens in attendance caught her attention for a passing moment, inducing her to wonder about the bandwidth of their collective ability to listen and actually follow. She snickered to herself about being gobsmacked by a burst of cynicism.

Closest to Lucy on the right was a young woman in a cut-down denim vest whose right arm bore a tattoo, the meaning of which was beyond, Lucy quipped silently, even the sharpest investigative reporter's ability to decipher. On the left sat a middle-aged man who probably had some lavishly tasty dish for supper, the redolent odour of garlic about him inducing in Lucy not only the thought that maybe she really was hungry but also the concern that maybe in her dash across Washington Square she did not completely rid herself of the reek of the hoppy craft beer she'd consume at the break in the conference.

"And now ladies and gentlemen, book boosters and poetry enthusiasts, and late arrivals as well," Mrs. Belle continued, voice rising as she held up the appropriate volume for all to see, "please welcome Isla Troyes who will read from her recently published *Furious Truths: A Memoir in Verse.*"

"Brilliant!" Lucy said.

At this precise moment, a phone sounded off in a musical rendition of *Hail, Hail the Gang's All Here*. The interruption raised an array of disturbed shuffles and disapproving murmurs. An old guy, looking like a garden gnome ornament—all that was missing was the pointy red hat— raised a hand apologetically.

"Just brilliant!" Lucy said, more to herself than to anyone within hearing.

Isla got up and slowly approached the podium, and with a subtle wave of her hand indicated that she appreciated the assembly's applause. Stuttering slightly, she thanked Mrs. Belle and thanked 4To Books for inviting her to appear in the same venue as Beatrice Beaumont, whom she called absolutely inspiring. She thanked friends and family and fellow students from NYU for all the encouragement they'd provided and for showing up that night to support her. Lucy identified Alexsis Troyes among those seated in the first row, giving her sister two thumbs up. The blond sitting in the chair next to the one Isla vacated Lucy identified as Candace Troyes, the student-cosmetician who, Lucy recalled, contrasted so evidently in personal appearance with Isla when they appeared together on the *Iphigenia*. There was no mistaking the blond hair. Eleni, Candace's mother, was there as well but there was no sign of Virgil Troyes.

There was definitely no mistaking Isla Troyes physically for other than the young woman Lucy remembered from her week on the *Iphigenia* and from the photos in the promo material gleaned off the internet, a brunette with a saddle of faint freckles over her upturned nose and washed-out blue eyes that could lead one to suspect that the absentminded gaze she occasionally affected was permanent. On the other hand, had the concentrated look of respectful vacancy, that Frank Veridis noted, morphed into stylish articulation? She obviously no longer shied away from makeup although she had not quite taken to Boho Chic. And what of that startling form-fitting red dress that clung to her? If the image of the muse Erato on the cover of her book had been purposely downplayed, then the opposite could be said of Isla's appearance at the podium as she held up the image for inspection: it was a kind of ironic reversal where what Lucy previously saw as plain about Isla, though not unattractive, was replaced by a more vibrant version of who she was. Moreover, active engagement had taken up where passivity had given over. Would that streak of self-assertiveness once observed in her become evident as soon as she started to read from her work? In her late-twenties now and no longer so unpretentious in her appearance as to hint that, just possibly, sadly, she was deeper than her awkward appearance might suggest. Looking around the audience before her, she seemed to project, as far as Lucy could determine, an understanding of just who she was and why she was there doing what she was about to do. Isla Troyes exuded confidence. She radiated a species of light emanating from deep within.

Someone at the back of the book store whistled loudly. A bout of laughter ensued and that allowed Isla to ease further into her introduction.

"Thank you, Flex, for that little extra bit of acknowledgement. Never had a cat call before. It's like a backhanded compliment, but something you take notice of nonetheless."

Lucy turned around immediately, identities mixing with remembered personalities racing through her mind. Flex! Yes, she remembered Flex from the *Iphigenia*, Alexsis' companion whose arrival was instrumental in bringing a smile to her face and a noticeable change in her demeanour. Called a knight errant in white runners and fashionable tracksuit, he somehow rescued her from the darkness that surrounded her. He also passed as a stand-in for MacHeath from *Mac The Knife* or, at the very least, he was definitely familiar with how a villain might operate even in popular song. It looked as though he had his arm in a sling. Lucy recalled that long lost Forrest Troyes was his companion from way back and his slash-dashing partner. In making that last connection, she wondered if Forrest Troyes were anywhere in the audience and looked about indefinitely with only a vague idea of what he might look like. When Isla picked up again, Lucy focused her attention on her.

"Now, allow me to introduce all of you to Erato, the muse of poetry," Isla said while holding up in her right hand *Furious Truths: A Memoir in Verse*. Pointing with her left hand to the box of books on the floor next to the desk, she added, "Erato's here in multiplicity tonight as Mrs. Belle pointed out in her own words earlier. Get on the wavelength of the muse. Erato will have you contemplating much."

After a quick burst of applause brought a smile to Isla's face, she proceeded to explain, "Erato operates in the world of creativity under the divine authority of Apollo. Like Apollo, the muse is traditionally presented with myrtle and roses, playing the lyre. In this rendering, however," Isla went on, her book held out before her and displaying the cover, "she is depicted as pensive, meditative, introspective. A perfect reflection of the themes I've attempted to explore in my poetry. It is a memoir and therefore autobiographical elements will rise to the fore. Family, friends, take from my efforts what you will but take nothing too personally."

"You go, girl," Candace Troyes called out, initiating spasmodic clapping. Here, Lucy made out the profile of Eleni, Isla's aunt and mother of Candace. Still as attractive as ever.

After acknowledging her cousin with a demure nod, Isla remarked, "I've borrowed from Dante's *Divine Comedy* the somewhat paradoxical need, and I quote, 'to put in verse things difficult to grasp.' Also significant for me is how Dante invoked Apollo to ensure his verse would be worthy of heaven's approval. For those of you forgetful of who's who in Greek mythology, please understand that Apollo is the god of music and poetry and the divine overseer in many areas of human concern, like justice. In his apostrophe to him, Dante embraces

Apollo's cosmic transcendence. I am less ambitious, I suppose you could say, but I remain hopeful."

Chapter 6
Omniscience

Truth be told, I did expect to be acknowledged at some point in the unfolding of this narrative, the reason being that I saw fit to infuse in Isla's general understanding of how inspiration occurs the need to recognize and proclaim my influence; however, I did not anticipate such a quick introduction and quasi-invitation to enter so immediately into the scene taking place in the 4To bookstore, one that put Lucy Hunter, star witness and reporter, on the periphery. Nonetheless, as it turned out my participation at that juncture was not only workable, it proved beneficial and resulted in the edification of all attendees and especially of those looking on later with reading glasses perched on their noses bent on following the action.

Isla's words proved enlightening enough but permit me to cast a little more light on the subject as all light is mine to share wherever I deem appropriate or necessary. An invocation is a more elaborate form of apostrophe: it is an address, very formal in its articulation, and often to a god; its meaning derives from the Latin *invocare*, which is to say, *in*, meaning *upon*, and *vocare*, meaning *to call*.

Permit me to elucidate further. I, really over the centuries, have preferred the concept of *deus ab initio* rather than *deus ex machina*, the benefits of which will become evident as the scene at 4To Books develops. And as to *in medias res*, it is a conventional starting point in grand works of the imagination dealing with historical and philosophical themes; thus and therefore, by this page in the book open before them, readers should pretty well know they are already in the middle of things and are well on their way to appreciating my *raison d'être*. The reasons for my being involved in the telling at all will become immediately evident and will be developed further in scenes that lie beyond the crowded confines of 4TO Books.

Thus and therefore, it is incumbent upon me, given my supreme status among the immortals, to oversee the present narrative as I've long been implicated one way or another in how events run their inevitable course, my actions often having been called prototypical. And by the same token, I've long been understood as the source of inspiration for all narratives, epic or otherwise. Consider Homer in *The Iliad* and *The Odyssey*, Virgil in *The Aeneid*, Dante in *The Divine Comedy*, and Milton in

Paradise Lost. That being said, don't expect excessive extrapolations or elaborate editorial comments full of justifications and empty rationalizations that can be construed as no more than a dangle of tangles. Just accept that I am yet again seeing to the marriage of truth and beauty. Should this prove problematic for average readers, let them consider me as no more than an omniscient narrator with all the literary liberties that this point of view has always sanctioned. *Tom Jones* comes to mind here. After all, they've got to this page without too much confusion or consternation and that, in my book, is quite encouraging. I absolutely refuse to let them lose the plot.

In the role of omniscient narrator with a far-reaching voice, I permit readers to get into the heads of assorted characters, feel what they feel, hear what they hear, smell what they smell, evaluate their thoughts and motivations, and ultimately approve or disapprove of their choices. To extrapolate further, I can present for those same readers what a short but curious character might consider doing to enhance her perspective in a given area, namely, slide a big, thick book off a bookstore shelf and sit on it, thereby literally elevating her physical point of view. This is an action she might or might not take. She'll decide in due course. Previously, a fat phone book would have been the riser of choice but in the contemporary world the phone book has fallen out of vogue in most jurisdictions even when available, which is highly unlikely, given the givens of the computer age. I can restrict impressions expressed to those of a specific character chosen to move the narrative along. Lucy Hunter comes immediately to mind.

Omniscience also allows for the opening of a new scene wherever it is deemed to be in keeping with plot requirements; for instance, describing a setting where books were everywhere, endless stacks of them, endless shelves of them, all coming across to the viewer with an eye for the exotic like colourful but novel wallpaper that professional decorators hung with artful precision. Crack a brand-new paperback open and the smell of ink on paper infuses the nose with great expectations. It is definitely within the remit of omniscient narration to intimate that a description might be excessive or a phrase might be bordering on the hackneyed and therefore be of dubious intellectual stimulation for the well-read. For instance, a diversified group being described as a "motley crew" unless the group in question is decked out in pirate costume as they frolic their way to a dress-up ball, or a band of Dionysiac revellers rollicking onto nature's dance floor in moves choreographed by professionals down at the rehab centre. On the other hand, said point of view also provides readers with descriptions that draw them in or entertain them in the way described video or enhanced sound in television programming serves mortals with restricted vision or impaired hearing or, possibly, a combination of both.

Therefore, in seeing my duties through to satisfactory resolution, I promise not to denigrate others of equal standing as mine, that is to say, my Olympian peers, and that includes those who in the recent past have attempted in their novel outpourings to put me down. I have always operated from on high, always taken to the higher ground, to use a metaphor often employed by mortals. I ascend eternally, and in the process bring those invoking my assistance along with me.

Ergo, back to Lucy Hunter and her observations and especially her propensity to establish a stable and trustworthy perspective. True, periodically she relies on ekphrasis, which involves describing the setting of a scene or a work of art so vividly as to have the reader not only see it but to virtually experience it. For this I commend her although she demurs when this particular talent of hers gets mentioned. From time to time I prompt its application, which is one of my favourite activities in effecting inspiration in creative mortals no matter what discipline they've embraced or what degree of modesty they assume when deservedly praised. Nothing entertains the demanding reader more than a solid block of description decorated with figurative touches, a parapet of purple prose, say, especially if it enhances linguistic appreciation or indeed inoffensive comment from either side of the critical spectrum.

Lucy admitted to indulging in apophenia, the propensity to see patterns in unrelated events and then draw conclusions. This I have observed in her with some pride and much of the time her hunches proved both revealing and relevant. However, with regard to what she decided at least tentatively last evening in her Beverly hotel room about the reasons for the murders that so affected Isla and Alexsis Troyes, Lucy might be in error. Then again, perhaps she might not be in error. She would be the first to declare that all mortals are capable of apophenia, for instance, seeing angelic forms in the clouds above and then speculating about beatific visions. Frequently what results is a potpourri of snapshots designed to elevate the claims of competing beholders, whether they be worthy of inspiring celestial illumination or not. In contrast, we immortals eschew the temptation to see the stern visage of Father Zeus in anything as mundane as a cluster of grapes or a rocky formation off the southern coast of Crete. Cosplay when applied casually to illustrious immortals like me or Zeus or Athena is most disconcerting.

This I confess to: I was instrumental in how Lucy, absolutely knackered, to use her expression, drifted off into euphoric restfulness while listening to Chopin's Nocturnes. Her contemplation of divine input, that is to say, her vision of my performance under the laurel tree, was born of her knowledge of Greek mythology, limited though it be, and impressions derived from viewing artistic renderings of my august self in grand exhibition halls like at the British Museum and the Louvre. Ditto for images of Erato. Significant above all this influencing and supposing is Lucy Hunter's driving need to separate fact from fiction and be responsible for establishing the truth and printing it when required. *Ergo*, back to her and by the same token, back to Isla Troyes at the podium.

Chapter 7
Furious Truths

Isla Troyes began. "My intention, I suppose you could say, was to encapsulate personal truths in this collection while avoiding sentimental excesses. For you poetry aficionados out there, my preferred choice of expression is blank verse. Iambic pentameter for consistent rhythm. I am not averse to rhyme and fall back on it for emphasis or in sonnets with a definite rhyme scheme."

Since Isla Troyes had named her collection of poems a memoir in verse, so the public revelation of those furious truths life delivered her, Lucy reasoned, would of necessity follow a chronological order. As was her wont, Lucy made a point of jotting down in her notes what she considered most revealing and helpful in building an accurate picture of the Troyes Family tragedies. It had definitely become an all-consuming puzzle to be solved. Isla's revelations would be insightful.

"So," Isla continued, "let me begin my readings with *Ode to Jenny Troyes*. This free

67

verse effort concerns a sibling who was unfortunately lost to the family, an older sister I never got to know and love."

Imagery in the poem developed around several allusions. Jenny was depicted as a princess locked away in some mythical tower of yore, kidnapped by a crone-like sorceress. Jenny's cries for help continued to fall on deaf ears. Unlike mythical Perseus, who succeeded in releasing Danaë from her tower and who went on to slay the Gorgon, Jenny's would-be saviour, the archer Gallant, failed miserably in securing her release. Jenny's ethereal voice would echo eternally.

While Isla read, her voice took on a dreamy, melancholy tone as if in need of solemn musical accompaniment. None came, of course. Lucy favoured rhyme and alliteration in poetic expression—what she called traditional, old style— but Isla used none in her first poem, which disappointed Lucy. She recognized a kind of Rapunzel figure and judged Isla's expression effective in creating setting and in moving the story along. But Jenny Troyes, unlike other heroines, real and imagined, never returned to her family.

"Sad," Lucy heard one of the natty hatted ladies say.

"Our father, Victor Troyes often took us kids on outings intended, we always speculated, to educate us. *Coney Island*

Escapades undermines that foolish childish apprehension. I'll read it now."

The poem concludes with a question: "Rides, slides, and pink fluffy candy, what could be more educational than that?"

Applause.

"Our father," Isla began again, "also took us to Greece when we were young, Alexsis who is right here, my brother Forrest who unfortunately is not here, and me. There was his business side to these get-away vacations, but that did not really interrupt the touring around all of us enjoyed and the usual touristy things we did, even our mother. May they rest in peace, Victor and Kat. The next few poems I'll read reflect that time in my life, in *our* lives. There is no chronological order to these poems, nor to any that follow. I'm just reacting to spur of the moment inspiration about what to read next."

"Hmmm," Lucy muttered.

And so, Isla launched into *Corfu, Fugitive Colours,* and *Island Hopping* in quick succession, smiling widely at the conclusion of each. In the latter poem, Isla through the use of repetition, with rhyme working overtime, highlighted the predominant colours in the Cycladic archipelago, blue and white. Delos, the island sacred to Apollo, figured prominently in the lines, the closing couplet describing the "terrace of the lions" as particularly uplifting. *Ruby Red,* on the other hand, evoked a sad memory of her brother Forrest spilling blood; the poem dramatized a metaphorical extension of a geometric pattern in its silver setting and underscored the "lovely sounds but cruel complacency" of an action with unintended consequences.

"On these vacations in Greece," Isla went on, flipping a few pages in her book, "we attended plays at Herod Atticus and at Epidaurus. Picture it. Centuries old open-air theatres, sitting under the star-filled sky, even the fireflies seemed magical. The hush then the explosion of ancient emotion echoing perfectly what goes on today. Absolutely wonderful, and even though we didn't understand a word the actors were blurting out, we knew the story that was unfolding in rather dramatic fashion because Dad always gave us the plot. I remember a play about what happened to legendary figures like Agamemnon after the Trojan War. All about justice and revenge. And bloodshed. Sometimes Dad would embellish things to maintain our attention and then, calling it all nebulous history, poke us in the ribs, especially Forrest who often appeared enthralled with it all."

Interpreting the Wind, Divine Dictates, Regicide, Matricide, and *The Erinyes* next presented Isla's audience with a five-part narrative elucidating themes of great popularity in the classical Greek period. It would have been obvious to informed listeners that Isla had done her research well; others less in the know might have been totally mystified but enchanted by the rhythms her lines delivered. Both sets of listeners might have wondered how these particular poems reflected real issues in Isla's life that induced the painful lament the title of her book posited. What personal truths, if subjected to close reading, would the poems reveal?

"Over the years of our visits to Greece," Isla continued, looking up from her book resting on the podium, "we saw all three plays of the *Oresteia*. To have witnessed in my youth the enactment of such bloody brutality was terrifying despite my understanding that it was all merely actors acting parts, realistic though the staging appeared to be. The last of the three tragedies eventually prompted me to compose *Furies To Juries*, which I will now read."

The poem dramatized how sanctioned by Apollo to avenge his father's murder, Orestes found himself trapped in a moral bind. With stark imagery, Isla draws out the conflict of two goods, one legitimate ethical principle clashing with another, but she leaves resolution of the conflict out of the equation implying that readers of this poem, or in this case, listeners, must take on the responsibilities of jurors.

When providing background for a particular poem or a thematically linked run of two or more, Isla had the habit of rubbing a silver brooch pinned just under her left shoulder. Lucy was intrigued not only by this habit— fingers long, delicate, supple— but also by the broach itself; it combined two distinct shapes, a clearly defined phoenix emerging out of a crock-like vessel. Close enough to see particulars, Lucy presumed the pot shape was more burial urn than crock and, given the symbolism of the piece, specifically the rising phoenix, it would have contained ashes.

Isla began in a huskier voice to read *Dire Announcement*. It was as if it were imperative she do this particular poem at this particular time, given the way she flipped through the pages of her book and then finally announced the title. While Isla read, Lucy's thoughts drifted back to events on the *Iphigenia* the morning Conrad Steele's body was fished out of the canal. She remembered Kat's unrestrained sobbing and moaning. She remembered Alexsis proclaiming what all her mother's grief and lamentation meant, it meant that she then knew "what we'd been suffering since our beloved father was killed." Lucy also remembered that someone on the scene opined that despite the high dramatics, Kat's reaction as a grieving widow was genuine. The poem came across as less dirge-like than moderated celebration.

At this juncture a bout of seemingly uncontrollable coughing in the audience just ahead of where Lucy sat mutated into a source of general annoyance—behind-the-hand comments, shifting positions, and shuffling feet. Isla waited patiently.

In *Trove of Hurts* Isla unspooled an elaborate, winding thread of regret that more or less listed with brief epithetic comment lost loved ones. *Grief* and *Good Grief* related how the killing of Victor Troyes affected her and her siblings. The imagery in the two poems conveyed the impression of endless weeping.

"Ah yes, this one," Isla remarked and grimaced, tapping a finger on the edge of the podium, "these fourteen lines reflect the mysterious demise of Cassandra Fortune, my father's close associate. How fondly we remembered Cassie at company picnics telling us what the future held by reading our palms or laying out and interpreting Tarot cards. She was adept at sortilege. Unfortunately, she did not see in the cards her own tragic death. So, to her memory, here is *Palms and Psalms* in the form of a Shakespearean sonnet."

"Dreadful, appalling," from another of the natty-hatted ladies in Lucy's vicinity when Isla concluded the sonnet with a particularly striking couplet.

Bonds of Love and *Bonds of Hate* sounded like echoes of each other and accounted for the feelings of the three Troyes children as they were forced to accept new realities in their young lives— father murdered and mother remarried. They were companion pieces, Lucy speculated, and noted the idea down in her pad that Kat and Conrad were the unnamed personages referenced not with deference but with less than subtle antipathy. When Isla continued with *Pathetic Poppa* and *Rad Dad Conrad* and then *Greed* in quick succession, Lucy's premonition about identities proved to be confirmed. She remembered how on the *Iphigenia* Alexsis talked about the situation Isla and she as teens found themselves in. They were choking on the smoldering embers of concealment and suppression. Alexsis resistance was a slow burn to begin with but out of the smoke and confusion of emotional and mental blackmail a raging blaze of animosity emerged. In Lucy's estimation, poems describing these sorrows and regrets did not quite measure up to the tone in the elegiac composition for sister Jenny or the lyricism of the poems featuring Victor Troyes as beloved father and literary tour guide.

"Dreadful, absolutely dreadful," the first natty-hatted lady was heard saying, expressing what many in the audience might well have been thinking as well.

In her note taking, Lucy attempted to scribble a phrase that identified the theme or intent of each poem; for instance, for *Rad Dad Conrad* it would be *Alexsis' intense hatred of stepfather*. Lucy's rationalization for doing so was that any such statement would have to correlate with what she already knew about Alexsis' recalcitrance in addition to not contradicting in any way what she remembered others having said about her, including family members. In proceeding this way, Lucy was again cognizant of how memories could merge and fuse and then do nothing but confuse. She proceeded mindfully.

On the *Iphigenia,* Conrad Steele made every effort to convince Lucy he was a nice guy and a loving father when Alexsis' repeated public display of resentment had threatened the equanimity of all the guests. The derisive rasp in his voice didn't make believing him easy. He had a cheerfully obnoxious way about him that gave over rather seamlessly to sardonic condescension. He talked at his listener in an English accent that Vanessa de la Croix derided as plummy rather than posh. Converting an irritating splurge of grievance against his son to a facsimile of grace was most amusing to those observing, given his normally arrogant and overbearing behaviour.

A series of sonnets with Isla's siblings as the main focus followed next. Among *Forrest Lost, Living in Isolation,* and *Slash Dashing Abstraction.* They confirmed in graphic imagery what Lucy knew about Forrest Troyes and how he had been ostracized. *Adventures of Boy Avenger,* which Isla read last among the poems dedicated to her brother, dramatized the marvelous machinations of a prepubescent fantasist. It was a somewhat longer narrative and self-sustaining enough to elicit appreciative snickers, contagious giggles, and one or two guffaws. This poem, Isla explained, was based on Forrest's immersion in his stack of Classic Comics amassed over a period of a few years thanks to the generosity of their uncle, Virgil Troyes.

Isla pointed at the woman in the front row sitting next to Candace and then nodded her head affirmatively, an attempt, it appeared, to convey both thankful recognition and awe. In hearing *A Low Burn* read, Lucy figured Isla was about to include Alexsis in a more direct and personal way. *Mourning Becomes Alexsis* struck a familiar chord with Lucy and with the reading of the poem her mind filled once more with multiple impressions and recollections, triggered by Isla's metaphorical 'scrapbook of sliced photos and bits of cleft recall mounted in collage:' Alexsis' dark clothing, her disconcerting behaviour, her private and intimate heart-to-hearts, her detailed email disclosures about life in a world dominated by Conrad Steele and all the *what if's* (locked away in cursed inaccessible files). In the poem, Alexsis emerged as a Boadicea, a Joan of Arc, a Medea. Noted well.

In her introduction to what she called the *Iphigenia* selections, Isla said, "Picture a tall individual standing tall at the top of a very high structure. Got it? Right. It's our very own Boyd Alexander Steele on the Pompejus Tower in Belgium."

"In Holland," a voice from the back of the room called out. Lucy turned and immediately recognized Boyd Alexander, Conrad Steele's son, standing a head above most in his vicinity. No mistaking him: dark eyebrows, pencil thin mustache, biggish ears, wavy dark hair. On the *Iphigenia* he'd been called a sad Clark Gable look alike.

"That's right, Boyd, Holland. A year or two ago, the whole family was engaged on a boat and bike excursion through Holland and Belgium. Our boat was the *Iphigenia*. In *Stalwart Softie* I recognize the influence Boyd Alexander had, and still has, on my life."

Lucy appreciated how the poem dramatized the father son dynamic, the inherent dysfunction of the relationship that was so evident each day of the seven day excursion on the *Iphigenia*. The concluding stanza of *Stalwart Softie* recalled in a most favourable light the karaoke scene onboard where Boyd Alexander sang Dylan's *I Shall Be Released* to the total dismay of his father. With the death of Conrad, Boyd Alexander inherited a fortune.

When Isla read *Coins for the Ferryman* her animated voice, at once literary and ordinary, trailed off in bemused reflection as if to suggest that the theme of this poem required deeper appreciation. *Affections and Antipathies* proved to be very subjective in terms of personal responses to old friends and individuals who met for the first time. Its humorous touches raised a few snickers from the listening audience. Self-recognition, Lucy determined.

Isla turned back to *Dire Announcement* but the woman sitting next to Alexsis down in the front row piped in, saying that the poem by that name had already been done. Lucy had no trouble recognizing Eleni, Candace's mother.

"Right. Okay then, two or three from the *Amaretto Algea*, the boat Candace and I sailed on during our second biking adventure in the Lowlands. *Caliban* is the name of this little piece. Some of you might recognize Caliban from *The Tempest*, believed to be Shakespeare's last play. Caliban is the nickname Candace and I gave to an elderly gentleman whose untoward and amorous advances toward Candace saw him suffer a fate he hadn't anticipated. He did his last walk of life over the railing and died in a heap. We felt responsible."

And that was the narrative that the poem delivered. It was as though Isla was holding back. She gave the impression upon concluding the poem that she should have resisted bringing up Caliban. She hesitated a little further and then flipped through the pages of her book.

"Heavy," Lucy heard one of the grey pony tail, bald pate gentlemen opine.

"This one," Isla said, rubbing her broach. "This is a hard one to get through but I'll try. *Legacy* deals with the death of Kat, our mother. It's a eulogy of sorts."

The imagery in *Legacy* was stark, less in memoriam than descriptive of the death kit Kat had at hand— needle, spoon, lighter, packet of powder, and the wailing that followed hard on the discovery of the body, arm extended awkwardly over the edge of the bunk, fingernails blue and somehow accusing. The last line of the poem states that Kat's going, no matter how, was like an antidote to her children's years of grieving.

Lucy recalled that it was indeed a lethal injection that did for Kat Steele and that her death was pronounced a suicide by Belgian police authorities. Then again, was it really suicide? That question continued to trouble Lucy as she was not satisfied that all facts gelled to form a totally satisfactory conclusion. No, there was something else. But what, precisely?

As to her own dealings with Kat on the *Iphigenia*, Lucy remembered, and not necessarily in a good way, that flummery worked best when engaging the woman in conversation. Kat, short for Katrina, was definitely formidable, imperious even, and could easily overwhelm listeners with her emotional effusions. What had Vanessa de la Croix called her? A well-preserved, middle-aged vixen capable at times of being elegant though not entirely into it too often. She had an air of theatricality about her and indulged herself in grandiose posing. If not portraying the role of forlorn wife and rejected mother her presence on the *Iphigenia* required of her then that of the bejewelled consort of a prince of commerce, employing all the stratagems of the distraught drama queen, the quintessential virago.

Kat possessed an austere kind of beauty. Patches of darker pigment crested her high cheeks and accentuated somehow her aquiline nose. Hers were full and nicely shaped lips that she licked often and pursed more often when challenged by Alexsis. She had lustrous brown eyes that sucked in all the available light when suffused as they could be with threat. If she was stressed or perturbed or angered or frustrated, her plucked thin eyebrows seemed to possess a will of their own, arching and falling independent of each other.

Lucy remembered hearing one of the *Iphigenia* guests opine that women like Kat Steele vanish into a cloud of superlatives, Botox and all the meretricious beauty resulting from its application notwithstanding. Many theories circulated among the guests concerning the character of Kat Steele, as many as circulated about Conrad Steele. Lucy could not remember ever seeing Kat Steele smile.

Isla pressed hard on her book lying open on the podium, seemingly trying to shake off the emotional exasperation that had gripped her during the previous reading. She fingered through a few pages, nodded, then raised her head and looked over her audience with a half-smile that indicated determination to finish well. "So," she said, her brow furrowed again, "I offer you *Urn* as a conclusion to my readings this evening. The poem is an enactment, an exorcism of sorts, an attempt to fix the past where it belongs, in the past. To accept the future as a benign unknown. And to live in the present, like at this very moment in this room full of books enlivened by the human interest that is so evident on so many sympathetic faces."

Isla read *Urn* with control and deliberation, her voice within the range she was capable of without sounding shrill or strident. It had been emphatic and convincing all through her extended descanting of life amidst family conflicts. Her delivery was anything but sonorous.

By and large *Urn* was a detailed description of the broach she wore at her breast, a phoenix emerging out of a vessel. While tuned into the rhythm of the lines, Lucy allowed her thoughts to drift back again to the *Iphigenia* the evening that Flex first appeared and gifted Kat with what became known as the wonky pink jug, which Kat thought of as ugly and inappropriate. When asked about it, Flex said he thought of it as the symbol for a new start, the new life she and Conrad had begun together after the death of Victor Troyes. He may have been engaged in doubletalk. Isla concluded her reading with a brief comment, one Lucy thought very insightful.

"This silver brooch was a gift from my sister Alexsis here and my brother Forrest who unfortunately, as mentioned already, was unable to attend. I love it dearly. I love them dearly. And I thank you all for your presence tonight and for your interest and your indulgence."

Applause filled the bookstore. The obvious positive reception of the budding poet pleased Lucy as much as it pleased the budding poet herself. Mrs. Belle joined Isla at the podium and embraced her heartily and then offered words of thanks.

"Such insight, Isla, such sweet sorrows so well expressed, such evocative descriptions of the heart's lament and the struggle to attain reconciliation. You have certainly delivered for us what the title of your book proclaims. May the furious truths of what you have revealed of your life in days past be transformed into earthly blessings in the days to come. May Erato guide you into a future filled with joyful accomplishments. Thank you, Isla, for your open honesty. And thank you again, Beatrice Beaumont, for your contribution to the evening's inspiration."

Another round of applause.

With Isla standing appreciatively at the podium, Mrs. Belle
waved a hand over the desk and then over two carton boxes resting on the floor on either side of it, top flaps open. She picked up a copy of a book from one box and then a copy of a book from the other box, held them out at arm's length, and announced in an ebullient voice, "Signed copies of our celebrated titles will be available immediately. Many thanks for your attendance here this evening at 4TO Books. Wine will be served shortly at the cashout desk. Enjoy, one and all."

After Mrs. Belle's closing comments, a general moving about began. An attendant pulled up two chairs into place on either side of the oak desk, Isla moved to the left, Beatrice Beaumont moved to the right. Lines formed. As Lucy made her way toward the wine counter near the exit, she observed Boyd Alexander (like a giraffe in search of leafy succulence) and Flex (in track suit) meandering down to where Alexsis and Eleni stood close to Isla, her head now bent, both hands moving efficiently in accommodation mode.

Chapter 8
Candace

While procuring her glass of wine, Merlot it was, Lucy's rucksack, hooked casually over her right shoulder, fell and hit the floor with a clunk. The young hippish man who had relinquished his seat, picked it up for her as he passed by.

"There you go, ma'am" he said and smiled.

"Cheers, mate," Lucy said.

"I know you," Candace Troyes said to Lucy, watching the young man as he headed towards the 4TO front doors. She then lifted her glass of red wine and inspected it against the light. She had full sensuous lips which she pursed in judgement. "At least I think I do."

"Yes, you do. We met on the *Iphigenia*, in the Netherlands."

"Like, two or three years ago?" Candace said tentatively. "The bike and barge tour, from Amsterdam to Bruges."

"Righto. Lucy Hunter at your service. Cheers."

"Yes, cheers," Candace responded.

"And you're Candace, Isla's close friend and cousin," Lucy continued, taking note that in the middle of her retroussé nose Candace still displayed a tiny heart-shaped stud.

"You know, I remember your earrings. My work requires me to judge appearances daily. As to accessories, I'd say your earring arrangement shines as a complement to your wire rim glasses. Very together, very ensemble."

"All part of the persona, yeah?"

"Exactly, I'm a blond through and through," Candace said after sipping some wine and nodding approval. She was nudged forward by an anonymous arm reaching out to pay the cashier.

Candace was a beautiful young woman. Her long blond hair was tied in a ponytail that hung down below her shoulders. Her complexion was olive-toned. Lucy pictured her in a minimalist Edward Hooper bedroom about to move to the window to view the city, slanted light a backdrop to her abundant nakedness.

"Fascinating group on the *Iphigenia*," Candace said pleasantly.

"International. From all over."

"There were these interesting older gentlemen we'd talk to at different times. Like, heart to heart, you know. It's not that Isla or Alexsis were looking for a father figure. Like, those older guys were just so

85

sympathetic and understanding. The ball cap guy, last name like a song or something."

"Cantor, Geoff Cantor," Lucy put in. "An observant, articulate fellow, so he was. He and I talked a great deal."

"Had something to do with filmmaking. The other's name was..."

"Veridis was the name of the other bloke, Frank Veridis. Looked like Sigmund Freud. Very witty, very candid."

"Right. He was, like, a professor or something. And you're a reporter, right? You had a sidekick, I suppose she was a sidekick, who took photos."

"Vanessa de la Croix. A proper photographer. Now in Paris, assigned to cover the opening of the Olympics. As for me, I'm here in New York to cover a conference at NYU on autocracy. All day today. I'm knackered again. Fortunately, I was able to catch Isla's reading. Completely fortuitous circumstances, I mean my being here right now."

"Fangirling like me?"

"Like you, yes. And like Alexsis and your mother, Eleni. Flex and Boyd Alexander."

"You have a good memory."

"Comes with the job, yeah? Right now, it's like the Troyes Family redux."

"Had their difficulties, the family," Candace noted. "It's on-going in a way. You still with the...the...?"

"The Bureau of Investigative Reporting. Yes."

"That's it. I learned over the week on the *Iphigenia* that you were a gutsy, determined woman who had been subject to death threats. Because of your job as a reporter. And that you wore sensible walking shoes."

"An accurate enough description, Candace."

"What'd you think?"

"About the threats or the shoes?"

"No, Isla' poetry."

"I thought it revealing. Not a cascade of colourful imagery but well-crafted. No expert, I. What was that line? '... the enduring taste of bitter lemons'?"

"Sting. 'Sting of bitter lemons,' I think. Isla told me earlier it was not her intention tonight to 'bleed suffering into a raw canvas.' Her exact words."

"Righto. I liked how she explained that her reading was not intended as, how did she put it, something like a vitrine for public display of painful emotion. Still, much was evident. I especially liked the Jenny poem. The sadness of loss, yeah? Isla conveyed that emotion well in the words she chose and how she arranged them and in how she read them."

"As far as I know, Isla's memories of Jenny are vague at best. As you heard, she was quite young when Jenny was around. Like, she wrote many poems over the years about Jenny, the sister she never knew. They say it was what started all the sadness and discontent. Always a princess captured in a tower in the wilderness and never found by family."

"Precisely. Got all that. I plan to get a signed copy of *Furious Truths* and maybe have a word with Isla about her work, maybe even with Alexsis, once the crowds around the desk diminish. Queuing up, always a bit of a challenge for me. Not so here at the wine bar. Luckily."

"We had hours in a line-up to get tickets for The Seamstress Quick Review Friday. Attending?"

"I'd considered the possibility, but her concert is not on my agenda, Candace. Unfortunately. And you're still into the world of beautification."

"Yes, I am. It's fabulous work. I've learned this about the job though, that not all clients treat you with respect. Like, some women look at you with total disdain."

"Hardly seems credible," Lucy said, shaking her head. "You strike me as the perfect model for what your industry promises."

"That's generous of you to say so, Lucy."

It was generous of Lucy to say so, but the compliment was not in the least insincere or helpless flattery in the face of human loveliness. And smiling at Candace, she remembered that instance on the

Iphigenia when Geoff Canter claimed that Candace Troyes was as beautiful as her mother, Eleni, and just as shapely, embellishing the impression by claiming she could easily have glided off the center of a Botticelli canvas, so startling were her green eyes.

Lucy detected in Candace's speech what she now recognized vaguely as a New York accent. Previously on the *Iphigenia* she had not thought of it as such; she just accepted the way she occasionally pronounced words as perhaps a speech impediment where vowels came into play or a way contemporary young women from America had of asserting themselves verbally through something as grating as up talk and voice fry. In the context of the Troyes family, the pattern was peculiar to Candace.

"Although I had contact with both Alexsis and Isla after the deaths of Conrad and Kat," Lucy continued, "especially Alexsis, I did not get all the details about the immediate follow up. I had a new assignment and had to get on with it. In Paris, where I reconnected by chance with Geoff Canter."

"Yeah, I remember you coming over to the hotel. One visit was, like, a virtual all-nighter. Odd though, that week in retrospect."

"It must have been a trying time for all of you. Police inquiries. Two deaths in the family. Finally getting out of Bruges."

"Yes, it was troublesome. Alexsis and Isla had the worst of it, and Boyd Alexander who was questioned a second time by that nasty cop. I think they even suspected him at one point of murdering his father. Boyd's now in a position of some authority in AEP. The company's under the guidance of Kinlaw and Archie Gallant. He's filthy rich, Boyd Alexander, a man of means now, as they say. But he's a decent, simple guy, really. Still loves his music bigtime."

Lucy recollected that Calvin Kinlaw had come aboard the *Iphigenia* accompanied by Archie Gallant, the one-time fiancé of Victor Troyes' daughter, Jenny. Not surprisingly, there would have been much for the lawyer to sort out. Crucial decisions had to be taken, some touching on the immediate catastrophes and others far-reaching in import, for instance, diverse inheritances.

"I always empathized with Boyd Alexander," Lucy pointed out after taking another sip of wine, "given the treatment he received from Conrad. My impression at the time was that the poor young chap had reason enough not to love his father, not at all. In dealing with Kat, he sided with Alexsis, if I recall correctly."

"I remember him calling Kat that hard bitch who replaced his mother. Sad, you know."

"At any rate, you all finally got away. Got back to America."

"Kinlaw saw to the arrangements. Official paperwork. Death warrants. Transport of bodily remains. Bodies transported to NY, even funeral arrangements here in the city."

"How did that go?"

"Well enough. Even poor Forrest was able to attend the funeral. Kat and Conrad were soon enough buried in a family plot, at some distance from Victor's. Kat wanted to be cremated. She once said to us all that she couldn't stomach the idea of rotting in the earth."

"She'd not be alone in that idea."

"I share the same repulsion, actually."

"Understandably. As far as Conrad's case goes, they arrested a suspect, didn't they?"

"His name was Dolf Van Handelaar. From what I was able to understand at the time, a lot of evidence kind of, like, put him in the picture."

"Right. Right."

"Strange fellow. Isla and I met him after visiting that exotic kind of museum, when we got lost. He directed us to Dendermonde where the *Iphigenia* was docked that night."

After a moment's thought and another quick sip of wine, Lucy continued. "I believe Dutch and Belgian authorities were familiar with Van Handelaar. He was a known drug dealer and petty criminal but not too swift on the uptake. He had form, however."

"Form?"

"A record of misdemeanours. Incriminating evidence was found in his possession, namely, Conrad's glitzy ring, his wallet and charge cards, and his smart phone. Loads of cash as well."

"And even the fancy sandals."

"And, as might be expected, a supply of drugs, including heroin."

"As to Kat's demise" Lucy said speculatively, "pretty much as the authorities determined? An overdose?"

"Suicide," Candace responded, her tone absolute. "None of us had any idea how she got the heroin."

"And the police?"

"Apparently they had nothing ."

"Did the notion of matricide ever come up?"

"What's that again, exactly?"

"Murdering your mother."

"Like in Isla's poem about Orestes?"

"Right."

"Not seriously. Sometimes people blurt things out when under stress but something like that in Kat's case never got mentioned. You know, Isla and I took another boat and bike cruise, on the *Amaretto Algea*."

"So I gathered from her reading. I wouldn't have thought you'd return to the scene of the crime."

"The idea was to get over all the negativity associated with the first time, the scene of the crime, as you say. An unfortunate death there too, the second time. Isla alluded to it in one of her poems."

"Caliban, yeah?"

"Poor bastard," Candace said, shaking her head ruefully. "Ah here is Alexsis leading the pack, coming to join us in a glass of Merlot."

Candace did the introductions. Lucy found Candace endearing, entrancing in fact, despite the plain way she had of expressing herself. Her cousin Isla was obviously the articulate one.

Everyone in the family group, including Boyd Alexander and Flex, remembered investigative reporter Lucy Hunter from the *Iphigenia* excursion through the Lowlands. Warm greetings were extended all around. This naturally led to Lucy congratulating Isla on the publication of *Furious Truths: A Memoir in Verse*.

"Your readings were particularly moving," Lucy said. "You must sign a copy for me before departing."

"Perhaps it is too much a self-portrait of existential misery," Isla confessed. "You actually get a different impression of what you intend when you hear yourself read what you've been at pains to write down in all honesty."

"Not at all. You girls suffered," Eleni said, rubbing Isla's shoulder affectionately. Eleni, statuesque in that generous way nature had determined, was dressed to the nines. So was Alexsis.

"You can say that again," Alexsis stated rather emphatically.

"Agreed," Flex and Boyd Alexander chimed in almost in unison.

Lucy observed at close range the bronze chess piece on Flex's jersey. She recognized it as the Knight from the Staunton collection of her youth and decided she liked it so displayed. She felt completely at ease in the Troyes group, and familiar enough with each individual to the extent that the two or three years since the *Iphigenia* experience seemed perfectly reduced to the immediacy of the moment in the 4TO bookstore. Another instance of time in her life being warped advantageously. She asked about Forrest Troyes but not much was forthcoming even from Flex who offered little more than a couple of shoulder shrugs.

After a polite ten minute back about a common experience, Lucy explained again why she was in New York, the conference at NYU on autocracy. She complained the day had knackered her and she needed to get back to her posh but not-too-posh hotel. She had a report to file by noon tomorrow.

Before leaving, she procured a copy of Isla's book, had it signed, secured it in her daypack, and made plans to see both her and Alexsis the next day for lunch. Bistro Massimo was where the three were to meet, a venue Isla knew as it was a couple of blocks away from her apartment.

Interviewing Forrest Troyes was a definite non-starter according to Alexsis, a great disappointment for Lucy.

In making her way along Beverly, not exactly skipping but not exactly tripping the light fantastic, Lucy heard in her inner ear the salutary strains of Beethoven's *Moonlight Sonata*. She likened it to soft light shining in the dusk. Before going up to her room, she took it upon herself to find a quiet corner table in the Four Square Restaurant where she pulled out her copy of Isla' memoire after ordering a light meal. She studied everything, front cover to back blurb, with the understanding that translating personal injury and pain and denial of personhood into vivid imagery presented a daunting intellectual and emotional challenge. As a whole, the work revealed much to Lucy, but she detected no discharge of venomous spite in any of Isla's poetry. Lucy felt herself beyond fatigued. It was time to retire.

Entering her Beverley Hotel room she stood silently before the mirror. The mirror was skint in giving back to Lucy anything she might have wanted to trade for. Answers to the questions she held back posing. She shook a fist at it, then waved at it more amicably because she understood its limitations, her limitations, and then turned away, dropping her daypack by the night table. She considered the somnolent light outside her window for a few moments, then sat down and turned off the television as soon as she'd turned it on. "Nothing but verbal wankers yanking out their points of view." That said, she turned the television on again and found the music channel she wanted.

Within a very short space of time, Lucy was soaking in her bathtub. She was drifting along, soothed by the consolation of mindlessness, the vagaries of human motivation sliding away like sudsy bubbles beyond her. Ethereal harmonies accompanied her downstream.

"Strident contrasts and atonal dissonance." She wasn't sure what she was listening to, Stravinsky possibly. Under normal circumstances, Lucy dripping with indignation told herself, she would not have described what she heard that way exactly, but then again, she certainly did describe it that way and cancelled the strident contrasts and atonal dissonance by turning off the television. Within seconds, she was puffing up her pillows.

Chapter 9
Harmonious Lyre

There is much to reveal about my expertise in the hallowed sphere of music. I am lauded for working my bowstring to perfect pitches and frequencies. As one of the adept declared ages ago: "Harmonious lyre: now the last string thou tunest to sweet accord, divinely warbling, now the highest cord." Be it understood, my mood is my mode.

Beloved Orpheus is the fruit of my loins and so is Asclepius, the former revered for his enchanting music, the latter for his healing arts. Without question, both inherited my talents. What transcends the mundane in life combines both; music and healing as one entity represents the most beneficial of gifts I have bequeathed to humanity. Alas, too often this generosity on my part goes unacknowledged in contemporary circles of so-called scholarship and analysis. Punditry is all I get.

However, let me proceed with my apologia. Modern theory discourses on the God frequency. It plays significantly within the gamut of all the healing frequencies. Fact is, the ancients uncovered its essential qualities, with my assistance, of course, in naturally accommodating environments. Caves, for instance. And in centres acoustically designed for hearing at precisely that level once the phenomenon was understood. Mortals in those long-ago times sought divine connection this way. They desired to be touched by the hand of their god. I am that god, as anyone possessing a profound understanding of the universe and all its diversity knows. Rituals evolved to achieve equilibrium and oneness. Altered states of consciousness in connection with sacred rites were induced. Tuning into the god frequency assisted in elevating mood or in relieving pain. Feelings of well-being and empathy resulted as well as changes in cognitive processing. Gregorian chant, a later musical innovation, delivered, and still does, such worthwhile health benefits, spiritual and physical both. My creative input, no doubt about it.

Modern research, with my assistance, subtle though it be, has uncovered additional advantages in mediating the god frequency. In favourable conditions, cell rejuvenation and regeneration occur. In addition, the right brain and the left brain, often working in opposition to each other, function as a unified force to stimulate memory, intuition, sensuality, spirituality, and imagination. Meditation, so embraced, delivers the mind holistic tranquility. Science measures access to the god frequency in megahertz; I measure it in levels of tranquility.

Humans in all walks of life, but those who read in particular, should give thanks to Hermes who presented me with his lyre.

Chapter 10
Mencken

The dream chasm, where unrecognizable figures emerge out of disjointed memories; a black hole of the psyche releasing in Rem-fired confusion everything it sucked in from yesterday, from last week, from one's entire life:

Lucy Hunter broke out of a startling dream and prepared herself to face the day. The ensuite mirror gave back a familiar enough reflection, pursed lips crowned with a frown and a lot of uncertainty in between. After her usual matutinal routine, she draped herself in the long cotton waffle bathrobe that the Beverley hotel provided, fussed again with the in-room coffee maker that registered with snarls and hisses its unwillingness to cooperate completely, and managed to produce a satisfactory cup of java, though what she really craved was a strong cuppa— proper tea, not the bland packaged blend left casually for the convenience of undecided guests. When in America, don't doolally, do coffee. Cup in hand, she dropped into the chair at the rolltop desk, almost tripping on the hem of the robe as she reached for her notebook stuck in her daypack abandoned by the night table. Before getting down to the real business at hand, namely, composing and forwarding her report on the previous day's autocracy conference, she jotted down the images she managed to recall from the dream that had launched her into daylight wondering.

Murky moonlight. A black knight rides across a red bridge. He is faceless under his visor. Waters in the foreground shimmer. Horse hooves resound, their echoes fade. Weaving shadows open to reveal the tumbledown ruins at Delphi. No clarity, no light. Pursuit by the dreamer proves impossible. A pillar topples. Blocked access. A scream. Waking.

Lucy's efforts to find meaning in these details met with failure. Too surreal to interrupt logically, but then again not surreal enough to confuse absolutely. The only red bridge she could remember was in Bruges. On a student trip years ago, she had visited Delphi and was moved to tears. Nostalgic fatigue rendered a bottom line: no more doodling as aide-memoire and no more dangling possibilities out there in la-la land.

With the requirements of her report in mind, Lucy proceeded to include the following from her wad of notes and decided that much of what she had scribbled down in the Take Action segment of the conference was, from an objective point of view, rather self-evident, such directives as maintaining separation of church and state, depoliticizing the democratic system, and protecting civil rights and voting access. The notion of "obliging the Fuhrer" stuck with her as a premise; she believed the phrase was prototypical of demagoguery and incipient autocracy. In fact, when the term was being bandied about at the conference long table, she reflected back on the totalitarian regime not only of Hitler but also of Mussolini, the latter leading her to revisit young Bert's story of brutal persecution and murder under the fascists. What was a paramount consideration coming out of the conference, and what she was determined to emphasize in her report, was the dire need on the part of reasonable people to understand absolutely that Roadmap 2.0 was already functioning full-on in the nation and that these same reasonable people must be prepared to take arms against it and by opposing, end it.

After sending the report to the Bureau, she entertained the ludicrous thought that a big decision faced her in what to put on for the day. Fact is, she had little to choose from, by default. When on assignment abroad, her motto was always travel light, be able to pick up and go at a moment's notice, pack limited attire, and so, one carry-on valise and a daypack. Her wardrobe for this sojourn in New York city amounted to three combinations for three days, travel time included; shorts, tops, a pseudo business combo of blazer, blouse, and tailored slacks, a sweatshirt bought in Amsterdam for changeable weather. She'd always taken pride in the fact that extravagance in attire was not her style.

Yesterday she donned the business attire and wished she hadn't. Today, the get-up would be suitable. To meet the Troyes sisters at the Bistro Massimo, where students hang out in droves, she'd go casual, shorts and a top featuring the face of James Joyce that she'd purchased in Dublin.

She dressed on the run, grabbed her daypack into which she secured Isla's book of poetry along with all the usual, and in the gilt frame mirror by the entrance caught a reflection of herself that left her mildly unimpressed, and banged the door behind her. She went immediately down to the Four Square Restaurant. The conference report was behind her now and so was the image of the faceless knight, the red bridge, and the ruins at Delphi.

She ordered a pot of English tea. As she chipped away at toast and marmalade, she mulled over the effects the dual interest her arriving in the city had foisted upon her. The forced elision of the two had by this point undergone a welcome caesura. With the report now out of the way, the Troyes Family saga would of necessity take precedence. Not that getting the word out back home about how Americans were responding to the threat of autocratic tyranny was of minor importance, no, not at all. She had complied with her assigned duty to inform the British public that totalitarianism could assume different personalities, different proportions, and be measured by different scales. One-size-fits-all was a near-sighted, delusional perception of political realities, local and foreign.

She poured herself more tea and turned her attention to the Troyes Family. She came to the conclusion that the fate of the family had already taken her in reveries beyond the professional remit her sojourn in New York allowed, but no mind, she could indulge herself in what was best described as pseudo-spontaneous entertainment. The time she had left was her own. Themes Isla Troyes presented poetically in her memoir had inspired her, inspired her to a point, that is. She'd already reached beyond narratives devised by Joseph Conrad or even E. A. Poe for recurrence. Such plots, recollected in anything but tranquility, had offered a kind of greenscreen of the imagination against which she had viewed and pondered certain family incidents dramatically played out in the past and which were being revived creatively in the present. Prompted by Isla's allusions, she even wandered into distant landscapes where tragedies authored by classical dramatists whose names she could not recall had what she playfully labelled priority billing. No, not quite, she did remember Sophocles, his *Electra*, studied in school. And *Oedipus Rex*. Hence, the torments delivered by the gods upon offending royal families, upon nobles of high standing and their misaligned descendants, or, viewing through a more contemporary lens, the curse of the rich and famous, both ancient and modern. It seemed to her at times that she herself had been cursed with unbound curiosity and that the light of understanding would never reveal the truth she so willfully sought. She felt driven by a force with a will of its own when it came to the fortunes of the Troyes Family, an impetus that had come over a day and a half to dominate her thoughts, an insatiable need to know. She looked forward to the luncheon with Isla and Alexsis where satisfaction would surely be attained. She hoped it would be an item on the menu.

Savouring the last of her tea, Lucy Hunter wondered how best to use the rest of the morning profitably. Strolling up Fifth Avenue to Central Park like a self-styled flâneuse, once considered a brilliant idea, was a non-started now with time a factor. Visiting the World Trade Centre was another option, but no, limited time. Returning to the 4TO bookstore was an option she considered reasonable. Bookstores were like magnets for her. She enjoyed the ambience. So much new info. So much stimulation. Like libraries, answers to mysteries hid in the stacks and beckoned you to come find them. She settled on strolling leisurely down Six Avenue to Father Demo Square, which was in close proximity to the Bistro Massimo. She would sit in the shade to re-read Isla's poetry and consider, possibly add to, the minutiae and marginalia she had already jotted down in the white spaces of the book. In dealing with Isla she wanted to ask pertinent questions and have those questions answered truthfully. Moreso with Alexsis with whom she would need to be more on the qui vive. At bottom, Lucy Hunter had an aversion to inconsistency and inconclusive denouements. Her reading started with Isla's *Furies To Juries*.

Pertinent questions regarding Isla's memoire faded the closer Lucy got to the Bistro Massimo. And likewise with the riveting mental need to have Alexsis reveal more about her *what if's*? Nonetheless, Lucy wondered if Alexsis would be willing to open up? On the *Iphigenia*, it was as if she had invited Lucy to assume the role of confidante. There, people weren't encouraged to tell *their* truth as opposed to *the* truth, the one true composite of unambiguous facts. Once engaged with her on the *Iphigenia*, Lucy did not say to Alexsis, "speak your truth." And the same applied to Isla and to Candace. To judge findings correctly, objectively, and without bias challenged Lucy Hunter's ability as an investigative reporter who demonstrated more than once the propensity to let personal or preconceived theory skewer final conclusions. She supposed that Isla in her *Furious Truths* expressed a species of subjective truth. It was a memoir after all. When it came to art in general exposing corruption and social evil in today's relativistic world of right and wrong where justice could be bought, Hogarth was still Lucy's guiding light. He had been for as long as she could recall her favourite artist and reformer.

Where to sit, inside or out? The long outdoor curbside dining shelter with its flower boxes and canopy looked as inviting as it had on her previous visits to the Bistro Massimo; today, however, an inside corner nook would be more suitable to intimate conversation that could, unless she held back, evolve into intimate interrogation. Besides, the ersatz terrasse was largely occupied by groups of students, some working away on laptops, some engaged in loud and enthusiastic debate. The small tables situated along the other side of the building's exterior, if pulled together, could seat three or four, but no, Lucy decided, not today. Inside. She would not deplete her expense account, she mused on entering, but she would not hold back in entertaining her guests either, satisfied in the knowledge that *in vino, veritas.*

Large windows on either side of the entrance brightened the interior of the bistro with copious exterior light. Bert was on duty when Lucy sat down at a corner table that she judged large enough to accommodate Isla and Alexsis comfortably. She pushed her daypack aside. No notetaking, she admonished herself. Besides not being necessary in the context she envisaged, scribbling away on a pad could prove extremely off-putting. It often had in previous interviews she'd conducted with potential informants, whistle-blowers prominent among them. No posing like a curator, yeah?

Bert greeted her warmly and she, him. Arriving early was not unusual for her when an arranged meeting was scheduled. Today, she had fifteen minutes to engage the young man she already admired considerably for any number of reasons, not least his pleasing, engaging personality and his perceptive observations that indicated wide interests and inherent intelligence. And, significantly, he had a sense of humour. She explained she was expecting two young women and while waiting would indulge herself with a glass of house wine.

"Red, please, young man."

"Yes, ma'am, Lucy," Bert agreed, pointing in an off-handed manner at her t-shirt.

"It's James Joyce."

"I knew that."

"I thought you might."

Bert bowed and retreated to the bar where he filled Lucy's order. It was a basic bar arranged simply with four stools aligned along its plain wood counter. Evident, the usual bar paraphernalia that included a hissy coffee machine, an array of purposeful glasses, and a display of wines arranged on ascending shelves. Providing a touch of the familiar and decorating two sides of a concrete column behind the bar hung photos and pictures typical of cozy and intimate eateries, of dubious aesthetic merit in most instances. A large wall mirror adjacent to the bar gave the impression that the place was twice as big as it actually was, giving the added impression that cozy intimacy was somehow diminished unless you found yourself in a snug surrounded by leafy adornments. The cacophony of a busy kitchen vied with the piped-in music that filled the empty spaces after tables were cleared and reset with cutlery and other necessities.

Bert returned with the glass of wine on a tray and presented it to Lucy with a slight flourish.

"Cheers, mate," she said, then turned to admire within arm's length an arrangement of potted plants reminiscent of Mediterranean greenery. She detected the scent of oregano. No, it was basil.

"My pleasure, Lucy. Did you make it to the reading alright? At 4TO Books."

"Yes, thanks for asking. I was a little late but I made it in time for the poet I most wanted to hear. In fact, she'll be joining me here. And her sister."

"Right on," Bert said, then excused himself. He disappeared outside and soon returned, his tray ladened with knives and forks, and cups and dishes.

"Is that Greek music I hear in the background?" Lucy asked when Bert returned from the scullery.

He looked up to the ceiling, to the overhead chandelier, as though consulting an in-house oracle only he had truck with. "Yes," he said, "I believe it is. We keep the music low key. Ethnic but subdued ethnic."

"Very good. Now tell me, Bert, what you thought of the conference on autocracy," Lucy asked after sipping some wine. She indicated approval.

"I was a little disappointed, actually," Bert said, shaking his head.

"Why is that?"

"Despite all the good intentions, all the information offered, all the caveats, no one among all the notable speakers emphasized the fact that elections have consequences. I know it's a cliché but, well, you know what I mean."

"That it's a political truism but factually true, yeah?"

"Yeah, exactly that."

"You can add into the equation that nobody among the speakers declared with any certainty the power of greed and fear in an election."

"Or ignorance," Bert threw in automatically. "Which is significant in this society. Crass ignorance. No one ever went broke underestimating the stupidity of the general population or the taste of the American public. That's from H. L. Mencken. If I had his book with me, I'd quote him directly."

"I've heard something like that before."

"You no doubt have and will again."

"It's all about exercising judgement, yeah?"

"The electorate has to exercise *clear* judgement. Many go to the polls with muddied judgement, others too quick to decide, still others don't vote at all either in ignorance of their democratic responsibility or because they judged the choices too extreme. I'll say this. Frequently enough you wonder what you actually get out of attending lectures and participating in seminars, but one thing I can say for certain, Plato had all this democracy vs tyranny conflict figured out centuries ago. Politicians don't read Plato. Some don't read at all."

"Plato was all about critical thinking, if I recall correctly. Had he today's buzzwords at his disposal, he'd have denigrated confirmation bias. I consider confirmation bias a comfortable armchair for the unthinking, for those incapable of critical analysis."

"Can work both ways," Bert interjected, "your confirmation bias."

"True enough. As a reporter, I try to get to the horse's mouth, so the expression has it. Sources matter."

"One of my profs offered this to chew on. That it is absolutely irresponsible of those at the controls of social media and the disinformation networks to foist false ideas upon a population all too willing to believe that two plus two equals five or whatever the math- challenged autocrat says it is."

"Sounds Orwellian."

"Right on. But I'm not really into doing a moral exegesis of a divided society," Bert went on, his brow knitted in an almost menacing way. "I'm not talking Doomsday scenarios. Not advancing the cause of preppers. But you get what I'm trying to say, don't you?"

"I do. Absolutely. In my report I put it this way: reasonable people must be prepared to take arms against incipient autocracy as defined in Roadmap 2.0 and by opposing, end it."

"Sensible people? Mencken also noted that sometimes the idiots outvote the sensible people."

"Righto, Bert, but not only in America. The future holds the answer, yeah?"

"Right. And the future is not far off, just a few months. Keeping to a holding pattern on the part of 'sensible people' is insufficient. The refrain of a Cohen song that I like reflects accurately what we're saying about the future: It is murder."

"Apocalyptic, so it is. Clear sighted. Agreed, sensible people must activate."

"You'd think, right? You know, I like to borrow the way Dickens began *A Tale Of Two Cities* when, as a native son, I talk about the two Americas. The best of worlds, the worst of worlds; the most advanced, the most regressive; the strongest in arms, the weakest in heart; so much in the hands of few, so little in the hands of many."

"Much to consider there, mate. But I'm keeping you from your duties. But before you get back to them, Bert, brain rot. What's your take on brain rot?"

"Essentially, it's mental and intellectual decline. From too much online crap. Or fluff, depending on optics. I have a touch of it myself because of my dependence on social media."

"Got it."

"You do?"

"I mean, I understand."

While Bert busied himself taking care of outside tables, Lucy sipped her wine and allowed herself to be distracted by contemplating the ornate chandelier that hung over the centre of the bistro. So much dazzling light. She counted up to one hundred pieces of pendant crystal before she felt a gentle tap on her shoulder.

Chapter 11
Isla

Isla Troyes was right on time as Lucy expected she would be.

"Hey," she said cheerfully, sliding into the nook.

"So glad you could make it, young poet of great renown."

"I'm high key now," Isla said smartly. The self-deprecation was obvious. She put her phone on the table and smiled.

"It's a lovely start, innit? Getting your first book published." Lucy tapped the tabletop rhythmically, a gesture of pleasing agreement. "And again, thanks for coming today."

"No problem, really. I like to be punctual. Alexsis on the other hand takes her time. These days she's involved in hugely important preparations for the New York Fashion extravaganza. Comes up in early September."

"Maybe she won't make it today."

"Not to worry. If she said she'd be here, she'll be here. In the meantime we can carry on."

"Right," Lucy said, pleased with Isla's assurance. She fiddled with her earrings then encircled her wine glass with both hands. "Have the waiter bring you a glass while we wait. Name's Bert. He's brilliant."

"Perfect," Isla said, and asked Bert, who had sidled up to the table, for a glass of what Lucy was drinking.

"And they don't serve plonk here," Lucy said, lifting her glass into the light.

"That's good to know. Lucy, it's great seeing you here in New York."

"Before making it to your presentation last evening, I attended a conference, as I may have told you already. Sent the report in this morning," Lucy said, seemingly glad to be getting that out of the way without delving into the details again. She nudged Isla's arm and added, "And it's great seeing you, too."

"Oh, by the way, Lucy, I have an appointment at two this afternoon. I forgot to mention that with all the excitement. Fortunately, it's local. Podiatrist, my hammer toe. Not terribly serious."

"We have plenty of time to chat."

"That's a portrait of...wait," Isla said pointing and nodding her head in what looked to be a sign of approval. "I do recognize that face on your t-shirt."

"James Joyce," Lucy put in after Isla hesitated to drop the name.

"I knew that."

"I'm sure you did."

"Your wine, mademoiselle," Bert announced, delicately sliding the glass of red into position on the table to Isla. "Enjoy."

"Cheers, mate," Lucy said, intending Bert as much as Isla.

"So you live in the area, do you? Green everywhere at this time of the year."

"West Village. Just off Bleeker Street. Near Commerce which is worth a stroll. Lots of history. The old theatre. I lay claim to very modest digs."

"And Alexsis?"

"Her apartment is on West 59th Street. Near Central Park. Not modest at all."

"Posh, is it?"

"Definitely. It's luxurious."

"Super," Lucy said and then after a moment's thought, added, "Like you, Isla, I appreciate simplicity. My flat's in Hammersmith, near the Thames. The landlord's a proper git."

"Git is universal."

"Aptly put. The tosser thinks I fancy him."

"Which means he fancies you, Lucy."

"Maybe, maybe not. I just hope he's fixed the drip, drip, drip in the loo while I'm away. So, Isla, a couple of years after the fact, I'll be enjoying the company of a published poet and an established fashion designer. The twists of fate that time delivers. Alright, then?"

"I have a long way to go. As to Alexsis' designs, they're slaps but a bit too culty for my liking."

"Slaps?"

"High quality, more or less."

"And culty, you say?"

"Appeals to those aspiring to be more than they are." Isla twisted her mouth a little out of shape. Duck lips resulted.

"I catch your drift. But she's enjoying a successful career."

"Very successful. Practically runs Excelsior State Creations. But like I said, her fancy designs are a bit too bougie for my liking."

"So bullocks to bougie, yeah? What about boho?"

"Even I can do boho and boho chic but as far as all that goes, boho glam exceeds my aspirations."

"Discerning, yeah?"

"True enough. You see, Alexsis' stuff is out of my league. It's uber haute couture. Even her Plain Jane line is over the top."

"So you go casual, but trendy, yeah? I noticed the ripped knees in the jeans you've got on."

"The ripped jeans thing drives Alexsis mad. Mostly she just looks me up and down and shakes her head."

"Taking the mickey, yeah?" Lucy said conclusively. She took note of the fact that Isla wore no jewelry save for the phoenix broach which was pinned to the collar of her blouse almost like an afterthought. "Studied casual?"

"You could say that. Thrift shops and consignment stores are providential. But don't get me wrong, Lucy. Alexsis is very supportive and always has been ever since we were kids although she says she's amazed by my, what did she call it, 'parading around in this demimonde of pseudo intellectual elitism.' Ironic, to be sure."

"I got to appreciate her very directed raillery when biking in Holland with your lot. As you know, we did get quite close, your sister and I, before and after the deaths in your family. Like with you, my associate Vanessa De La Croix experienced a rough time of it growing up. While on the *Iphigenia* she shared my concerns regarding both of you. Very empathetic, so Vanessa is. She'd understand the suffering you describe in your poetry and how you express it."

"My brother Forrest suffered the most."

"You alluded to his isolation in several of your poems."

"I'm several years younger than Forrest. But he always seemed to me like a troubled, lost soul. Alexsis and he were closer. At least when he was around, which he was and then he wasn't. She's in constant contact with him now."

"How did Forrest get by over the years being cut off from family?"

119

"A trust was set up for him by Calvin Kinlaw, the lawyer, to ensure that he lacked no necessities. Virgil's influence, I'm sure. College expenses were covered as well. The funds kept flowing in as long as Forrest stayed away and made no outlandish claims about what he thought was his by right. Anyway, that's what I understand."

"Your brother was like a remittance man," Lucy commented, "cut off from inheritance and sent abroad on a fixed income. I found it interesting how your poems describe his absence and how it affected you. Brillant."

"Thank you, Lucy. You know, I had to get over my nervousness."

"You were absolutely poised. And there weren't too many distractions to put you off. At least that was the case when I was in attendance. Some great poems, yeah? So, good on you."

"Thanks again."

"To tell you the truth, Isla," Lucy said, playing with the rings in her ear again, "I've been through all of your poems a couple of times. Very stimulating. Some subtle effects. I thought your use of juxtaposition and apposition was super. In addition to the poetic devices you employ, I mean, like rhythm and rhyme and so on. Readers of poetry would take these for granted I should think. Not easy creating an autobiographical account of one's life in verse. Commendable. Brilliant, really."

"Even though illusory impressions can emerge from memory, I had no fear of creating a self-absorbed mental fantasia, no fear of producing for public display a disingenuous but suffering self. But my version of inscape, I suppose you could say.

"Metacognition, part of the process, yeah?"

"Yeah, that, and the history of a family, my dysfunctional family to be specific, and my place in it. Forrest and Alexsis, too, of course. And especially about what happened on the *Iphigenia*, you know, with its complete reversal of expectation."

"Tragic indeed, Isla. Wasn't the *Iphigenia* adventure supposed to be a positive family experience, bringing all of you together in pursuit of common goals?"

"Ideally yes, but Alexsis put the kibosh on all that, didn't she? You all witnessed her antics, didn't you? She got us all on edge, and then those freaky deaths. She had us younger ones gather in the lounge first night out."

"Yes, go on."

"Well, okay." Isla pulled herself up into a more upright position on the bench and casts about the interior of the bistro as though in an effort to collect remembered impressions. She smiled demurely and proceeded to explain. "Alexsis was there when I arrived. A moment or two later, Candace appeared and posed. A classical statue totally out of context. Then Boyd

Alexander emerged out of the shadows plugged into his music. Even in his awkwardness he towered over Alexsis. We gathered around one of the low tables 'to talk things over' as Alexsis put it. She told Candace and me to turn off our phones and Boyd to unplug. Why all the stealth, I wondered."

"Fear of being overheard?"

"Maybe. That Canadian guy was sitting at the bar when she started. He did his darndest not to eavesdrop, it seemed to me, but he could not help overhearing what we were saying, at least until he left. Nice guy, really. We got to know him better than the other cyclists."

"Geoff Cantor."

"Ri-ight," Isla said, appearing as though she were about to yawn. "Into film making or something like that. Anyway, as usual Alexsis was totally sceptical about the trip. She tried to convince us that 'this family fantasy' as she put it was organized by Calvin Kinlaw on Conrad's orders. It was all bogus. She believed the boat and bike thing was just another attempt to settle her down, to control her, to shut her up with distractions."

"Along the way Alexsis conveyed the same complaint to me," Lucy said, raising a finger in confirmation. "Basically, that the trip was to bring her around to finally accepting the situation for what it was, to have her make peace, as it were."

"That was her theme for sure. Had been for ages. When she mockingly accused me in the lounge of being too passive, too forgetful, too easily played, I asked what we were all supposed to do then. I was getting exasperated, you know."

"Understandably."

"Absolutely nothing was her answer to what we were supposed to do. Then she implied rather smugly that Kat and Conrad's plans for keeping control of us could easily get screwed up. I had no idea what she meant and she didn't explain."

"In such close quarters, you take in things not necessarily intended for your ears, yeah? I overheard a heated exchange in the corridor between your mother and your sister. She was berating her for constantly appearing in black and for stomping off petulantly and returning to the *Iphigenia* well after midnight."

"They'd probably been drinking. It became quite obvious to anyone observing her that Kat got into her cups quite readily. As you say, close quarters. Her happy hour started early and ended late. Same pattern for as long as I could remember."

"The tragic loss of Jenny," Lucy began again after a moment's thought, "do you think that might have contributed to Kat's dependence on alcohol?"

"Likely. I think Conrad was of that opinion. Consolation without real solace. You know, the older I got, the more convinced I became that Kat took Jenny's abduction very hard. She'd resented how our father dealt with the kidnapping and ransom demands. As kids we became very aware of the animosity taking root between them. Kat's rage was unrivaled until Alexsis came of age."

Isla broke away from her narrative. She allowed herself to be distracted for a few moments by Bert toing and froing across the central area of the bistro, delivering an order to one table and removing plates from another. "It's like he's doing ballet for our entertainment," she said, turning back to face Lucy and miming dance movements with two long fingers. "Great style."

"Agreed. Now in your other Jenny poem," Lucy said, getting Isla back on track, "one you did not read last night called *Daughter Lost*, you define Kat's sadness as contagious and describe how it affected you and the others."

"To be perfectly honest, I'm really quite vague about the depths of Kat's sorrow, I mean really, being younger than Alexsis and Forrest. When it was all shaking down, I mean. Like, I wandered alone into the realm of fantasy regarding a more sympathetic much older sister called Jenny whereas Alexsis could be moody, often unresponsive, and unpredictable. Her arms could bring you comfort and her tongue could cause you pain. As to Kat's lament, I did occasionally over the growing-up years espy her weeping over photos of Jenny's high school graduation when she thought no one was watching."

"Therefore the creation of something like *Ode to Jenny Troyes* which we heard last night. In reading that poem, your voice became melodic in tone, I thought, which was not evident in most of your readings."

"I believe I was trying last night to simulate the ethereal voice of my idealized Jenny, the tragic heroine of the piece captured forever in the unassailable tower."

"You present her in the guise of a princess."

"Makes sense. Her father was a prince. Our father was a prince. At least in the collective imagination of his three remaining children he was before we lost him."

"The poems dealing with your father Victor Troyes are numerous, far outnumbering others developing a particular theme."

"Hundreds attended memorial services for him. Virgil Troyes' eulogy moved many to tears. Forrest, Isla, and I were absolutely inconsolable."

"And your mother, Kat?"

"In her manifest grief, she sought and received sympathetic understanding from Conrad."

"So, a great loss, your father?"

"It's a mixed bag of emotions where he is concerned. Fond recollections and sad ones. What lifts me up is the knowledge that he was a loving, kind father. What brings me down is the vague understanding that his death was not accidental. As you may know, he was CEO of Advanced Electronic Processing before he died. I've always thought the motivation for eliminating him was internal, an inside job, as they like to say, company rivalry and so on. Police inquiries lean toward that interpretation of events although no definite conclusion was ever arrived at officially. Alexsis was never of that opinion. Nor Forrest. They had other theories."

"Like what?"

"That Conrad Steele was behind it." Isla glanced quickly at her phone. "Even our very resentful mother. I have a vivid imagination but that's too much of a stretch. It remains for me a mystery."

"Yes, I can see that," Lucy said, then indicating Isa's phone gyrating impatiently on the table, encouraged her to check out what she presumed was a text. Isla did just that, leaving Lucy to her own speculative thoughts.

"Message from Mrs. Belle," Isla explained, placing her phone back on the table, "from the poetry reading. Nothing extra exciting."

"Tell me about *Palms and Psalms*."

"I wrote that sonnet in memory of Cassandra Fortune who died shortly after my father was killed."

"Right, his personal secretary at AEP."

"Exactly. We loved her. She'd read our fortunes holding our eager hands gently in hers, tracing lines and interpreting them for us. And Tarot cards. How deftly she could manipulate the cards and lay them out just so in relevant patterns upon the table. Like, I remember the sound of her voice even today, how she calmly explained things and what juxtaposition meant."

"Suicide, was it, that did for her?"

"So official reports say. I think the death of my father affected her greatly. Alexsis thinks differently, has done so all along. She's under the impression that the two deaths, a mere week apart, are connected in some sinister way. Same with Forrest, I believe. Hard to determine, really. Know what I'm saying?"

"Yes, I understand completely. Your poetry does both of them justice. Regret was evident in your voice the way you read *Palms and Psalms*. At any rate, Isla, it was nice that both Boyd Alexander and Flex showed up for you at 4TO Books last evening."

"Yeah, Flex is great. He and Alexsis are an item, sort of."

"That's brilliant. I remember them being close while on the *Iphigenia*. Old MacHeath from *Mac The Knife* himself."

"And Boyd Alexander came too. I have a great fondness for him. What he had to put up with from Conrad. And he survived whole. He's supremely well-off now."

"I did witness the one-sidedness of the father-son relationship. The incident in the *Iphigenia* dining room gave me pause, gave all of us pause looking on. I refer to Conrad's pulling the chair back way too far so that Boyd-Alexander would collapse, which he did."

"He let out a mouthful of curses. Like, he wasn't too happy about what Conrad did."

"We wondered if Conrad's apology was sincere and whether his intention with the chair was to put the lad in his place and shame him at the same time for some indiscretion. I remember embarrassment registering on Kat's face. And a restrained kind of anger registering on Boyd Alexander's."

"Boyd always resented his father's treatment of him. Candace, Alexsis, and I tried to assuage his grief after that mean trick and in light of other nasty treatment he endured. However, there is more to Boyd Alexander Steele than meets the eye. He's gentle, and anything but soft, if you catch my meaning."

"Righto, not to be taken for granted. I thought he effected a subtle kind of tit for tat the night of the *Iphigenia* karaoke session. His rendition of Bob Dylan's *I shall Be Released*, I mean. He was really into the lyrics."

"I remember vividly how he held his audience completely spellbound?"

"Yes, and I also remember Conrad's reaction. He was vexed at what Boyd Alexander was saying through Dylan's lyrics. If looks could kill..."

"Exactly. Strange, how the day after there was a killing and Boyd Alexander *was* released. You know, the authorities scrutinized him in a very threatening way."

"Logical enough, their questioning him intensely," Lucy said decidedly. "He'd have most to gain by the death of his father, Conrad. Now, your poem about him—what's the name of it again?"

"*Stalwart Softie.*"

"That's it. Very revealing. He's succeeding now where he balked before, I suppose."

"He is."

Isla watched Bert pass by carrying several plates of food balanced expertly on his left arm. He pivoted and then backed his way through the front door. A burst of noisy exuberance from somewhere out on the canopied terrasse followed immediately. When Bert returned and headed towards the kitchen, Isla raised an index finger to her moistened lips and pressed it on the tabletop with a little bit of pressure. With contact she issued a quick hiss and jerked the finger up above her head. "Hot. So hot. I'd recognize him from behind anywhere."

"Not only hot but also smart," Lucy said, acknowledging Isla's animated show of admiration.

"Did you know," Isla asked, turning her attention back to Lucy, "well, I suppose you do, that Conrad Steele took over as head of the AEP corporation that our father once directed so successfully? Then he married our mother. Forest and Alexsis always maintained there was hanky-panky going on between Kat and Conrad long before Dad died, but I never cottoned on to what they meant until I was in my early teens. It added to their suspicions about how Dad died. Things were much better for the three of us when my father was around, especially for Forrest who, I admit, did have his issues. But who doesn't have issues?"

"What issues?"

"Alexsis is more up on the subject. Ask her about it when she arrives."

"Will do."

"Alexsis was always suspicious about what happened to our father and all the rest of it. As she got older, she voiced her opposition, powerless as she was to do anything about it. Like, they just laughed her off. There's a line in Shakespeare's *Hamlet* that goes this way: 'The funeral baked meats did coldly furnish forth the marriage table...' It reflects perfectly what Alexsis and Forrest said about all these new arrangements. Forest reminded me of that line before he disappeared. He's more literary than Alexsis.

Was always reading. Always into thought-provoking literature, even your Jame Joyce there."

"That's revealing," Lucy observed. "Now among the two or three poems in your collection referring to your stepfather, *Rad Dad Conrad* seemed the most incisive. The line 'no birds sang, no bells rang, and nobody brought a rose of any colour' conveys how unaffected you were with his death, strange though it was, and how dramatic Kat's reaction to it was that morning in Bruges. I marked those particular words in the copy you signed, so they're more or less fresh in my memory."

"Plainly, we did not mourn his passing. Nor did we dance on his grave. Only Kat mourned that morning, endlessly until she ran out of breath. Alexsis was of the opinion that dear old mother, so overtly overcome with grief, overplayed the whole thing when Conrad was discovered. The sort of eulogy for her that I call *Legacy* is more descriptive of how she did herself in than heart-felt lament, the death kit they found in her cabin as symbolic of her hopelessness."

"The last line of that poem suggests that Kat's departure, no matter how, was like an antidote to her children's years of grieving. I marked those words as well."

"For her, I did mourn. Admittedly, more than Alexsis. To tell you the truth, it's hard to know how Forrest took it. He's hard to figure out a lot of the time." Isla shook her head, sipped some wine, and went on. "I don't think Kat ever really loved us. Maybe the loss of Jenny had something to do with that."

"So you're convinced that it was suicide."

"The evidence is incontrovertible according to police authorities in Belgium. Who am I to disagree? I just don't know how she could possibly have got the heroin. Another mystery as far as I can determine. Here Alexsis and I agree. It's a mystery."

"Sad, though, yeah?"

"Very."

A sudden rattle and clatter from the scullery area followed by a bellowing outburst sent Isla and Lucy into fits of laughter. Lucy managed to spill what remained of the wine while Isla held on. Lucy accepted the levity for what it was, a natural, spontaneous break from what was driving her to know the facts from every angle possible.

She was beginning to feel as though she were asking Isla to pull apart a harness of complicated emotional wiring that she had already woven into a coherent exposition in her book. But she felt impelled to press on. She certainly recalled that it was indeed a lethal injection that did for Kat Steele and that her death was pronounced a suicide by Belgian police authorities. Then again, that nagging question: was it really suicide? That question continued to trouble her as she was not satisfied that all the available information on Kat's death gelled to form a totally satisfactory conclusion. No, there was something else. But what, precisely?

Lucy did not feel like a reporter whose job it was to ask relevant questions, exactly what she was, but a research assistant interviewing a literary personage, exactly what she was not. So a change in tack, though not exactly a change in substance.

"I noted that you were really into ancient Greek myths and legends. And the tragedians who dramatized them. Your *Furies To Juries* poem I found very intriguing."

"I based it on the last play of Aeschylus' *Oresteia*."

"I'm lost when it comes to all that classical stuff. I remember Zeus and Apollo but that's pretty much it. Oh, and the idea of the muses. Also your Erato. I'm a pedestrian writer, mind, not a poet or novelist. Wait, no, I know the Oedipus story, his conundrum and curse. Freud's influence, yeah? Also, I had to study a Sophocles play once. Enlighten me, Isla."

"That I can do," Isla said, nodding affirmatively. "Okay, sanctioned by Apollo to avenge his father's brutal assassination, Orestes was forced to contemplate actions not sanctioned by the deities of old who still held considerable power and influence. These were represented by the Erinyes who hounded him relentlessly and drove him mad over providing his mother with an unexpected quick exit stage left. Eventually, his case was heard in a court where Athene, goddess of wisdom, held the gavel. Hence, my *Furies to Juries*."

"Who's to decide, yeah? Who's attentive enough to grasp fully the meaning of Orestes' dilemma?"

"His dilemma can be viewed in the wider social spectrum, like on a continuing historical basis. As Tennyson wrote: 'The old order changeth, yielding place to new.'"

"Fortunately, matricide is not integral to the transition. Political assassination, yes, matricide not so much."

"That's almost funny, putting it that way."

"Not intended as comic relief," Lucy said, unable to hold back from snickering slightly. "Suicide is that other consideration, innit? Now, as far as you know, Dolf Van Handelaar bears responsibility for murdering Conrad Steele. That the case as far as you see it?"

"Dolf Van Handelaar. Yeah, Mr. Van Hoodie. That's what Candace and I called him because of the hoodie he wore."

"Candace told me she remembers how you met him and where."

"Right. It was at the Kunst Woestijn atelier — I think it's called that. He asked if he could help because we looked lost. His English was pretty good. A strange character as I remember. He had a scar on his cheek and tattoos on his arms and a death's head ring on a finger of both hands. It was almost as if he knew who we were and, like, where we had to cycle to. He did guide us to near where the *Iphigenia* was moored for the night. We offered him a few bucks in coins we had and some euros for his help, and he took it all willingly. He offered us some marijuana which we did not take and his offer of heroin we definitely refused. He must have been a pusher as he seemed to be travelling around in one of those large cargo bikes that was full of camping equipment."

"Candace said the evidence against him was pretty convincing. She's pretty sure he did for Conrad. What do you think?"

"I think she's right," Isla stated after giving the question some time to sink in. "But I have not followed up on any trial or anything over there. None of us has. Maybe Kinlaw, our counsel in a lot of ways. We just left all that back in the past although Candace and I did take another boat and bike excursion in Holland. Some poems in the collection reflect our adventures on it as well as our misadventures."

"Candance mentioned that to me last evening."

"How's the wine?" Bert, suddenly appearing, asked.

"Suits my impatient palate fine," Ilsa replied agreeably before taking a last sip.

"We'll have a bottle of it with our meal, when my other guest arrives. Cheers, mate."

"Yes, ma'am," Bert said and backed away.

Isla raised her eyebrows in looking at Lucy as much as to say: pretty interesting guy, what do you think? She then turned toward the door and said, "I'm sure Alexsis will be along shortly. In the meantime..."

"In the meantime," Lucy interjected amicably, "you and I can continue discussing your impressive book. I thought the cover very clever, totally in keeping with the general tenor of the poetry, as you pointed out to your listening audience last evening. Erato, the mythological Greek muse, who inspires poetic and musical creativity, captured in the very guise of contemplation. You were very clear and explicit in the introductory comments. What you said about Apollo added to what little I knew of his influence. Like his direct role in the service of justice. And then alluding to Dante and connecting the two. Brilliant."

"As you probably know, there are nine muses. Calliope is the muse of epic poetry and Melpomene the muse of tragedy. Dante labelled them 'Ladies of the Heavenly Spring.' As I mentioned last night, Dante invoked Apollo to ensure that his verse be worthy of empyrean approval, that he be worthy of wearing the coveted laurel garland. I was content working with Erato, if you see what I mean, although, metaphorically speaking, she was aiding me under Apollo's supervision."

Chapter 12
Delphi

Pardon the interruption to this informative, if not stimulating, exchange between Lucy Hunter and Isla Troyes. A point the poet raised with the reporter requires further clarification. Yes, there are nine muses, one of whom Isla mentioned as being of significance service to her, namely, Erato, and she referenced two others en passant, both dealing with grand versified narratives. All nine muses are the issue of Father Zeus and Mnemosyne, mistress of memory; they are not my daughters, as has been believed at one time; I am simply their *Musagetes*, their musical director, as it were, providing direction where direction is needed.

Be advised: I cannot account for all the distortions of fact that history delivers nor can I control the disinformation perpetrated in the contemporary world by those with malicious agendas to enact, those full-in-your-face tyrants and autocrats and would-be totalitarian rulers. Both Lucy Hunter, investigative journalist par excellence, and Umberto, aka Bert, garçon sans pareil at the Bistro Massimo, would appreciate my disclaimer, given their political perspectives. Though I have the gift of prophecy in abundance and can predict the future in certain instances for certain individuals with the right credentials and the right inclinations, I cannot control the past. My ambit in this regard is advancing truth, prophecy notwithstanding.

Take Delphi. Before excess wrought its ruin, that renowned holy place was associated with my name, and rightly so. Many versions are extant as to how I became *the* pre-eminent force there, some close to accurate and factually verifiable if the right authorities are sourced, some apocryphal with dubious attributions. Let it be known universally that I gained ascendance through my intellectual acuity and my invincible ability as an archer. My aims were always true. Moreover, Mother Earth recognized my superiority in all areas of jurisdiction that I laid claim to. And let it be understood unquestionably that Delphi was not my only shrine. Sanctuaries where my prophetic insight rendered truth were ubiquitous; my votaries, many, including hooded priests and gray-haired virgins. My instruction to those pleading for assurance about the right path to follow, no matter at what site they knelt, was to observe faithfully the will of the gods, to make peace with their designs, whimsical though they could be at times, and never to presume more than was reasonable lest hubris bring down the punishing hand of Nemesis upon the fat heads of those inquiring to know. Or equally painful, invoke the endless, wrathful pursuit of the Erinyes. Primarily, I urged supplicants to know themselves and above all to entertain nothing in excess. As to Delphi in particular, it was acknowledged as the centre of the world for an extended period of time, the omphalos there its navel. Within the confines of the sacred chasm the tripod of mantic revelation always delivered.

Don't presume that I am limited to alluding to the likes of Plato for substantial recognition. Remember: It is I who inspired him and his ilk with transcendental thought and a whole lot more. I who influenced his world view. I who projected the shadows on the wall of his cave. I who inspired him with the beginnings of a psychological understanding of human nature, certain as I was that discursive analysis was limited even when delivered in dramatic dialogues later defined as Socratic. Innumerable be my praises: for example, in high drama of epic proportions, and especially in lyrical overtures and declarations. To wit: "Apollo, whose locks are gold, whose oracles are sure, whose omens good reveal, whose precepts are pure. Divine Apollo, overseer of the world's wide bounds, who stamps the globe with forms of every kind and from whose lips no false word falls."

Firm in the knowledge that self-adulation in this context is not excessive, I am moved to include the following exalted note of recognition expressed as an evocative panegyric. "Your arrow is steeped in the honey of prophecy, feathered with the oracles of the fathers. Your bow sounds strong with your father's virtue; it strings powerful with miracles; they have killed the old snake through their own death."

In terms of the present narrative, I prophesize that Lucy Hunter, our central intelligence in this evolving narrative, will be rewarded in her pursuit of truth although what she comes to understand will require more of her and that will necessitate extensive research taking her beyond locating hidden passwords. My direct involvement, yes, assuredly. Always. But let me add that over the centuries I have learned to delegate, and the nine Muses have followed suit, deploying minions like the Naiads and the Nereids, nymph-fired inspiration with surprising results in the lyrical expression of all genres. Like light itself, which is everywhere except for where it is not, I am everywhere all at once except for when decidedly absent or simply in repose, and no philosopher can deny that even darkness is a testament to my eternal presence. However, in the case of a false flat (the term used by mortal cyclists to indicate a deceptively straight run will require more push power), not all aspirants are deserving

of a direct infusion of creative energy from
me. I delegate. Hermes is a superb surrogate.

Chapter 13
Buzz Kill

Arriving at the Bistro Massimo in uber style, Alexsis offered the following greeting: "Hey, you two, so heavily into your little tête à tête!"

"Fashionably late, as usual, Alexsis."

"All good?" Alexsis inquired, pulling in tight behind her the smart pleated culottes she was wearing. She shuffled in comfortably next to Lucy and arranged her purse. She sat directly opposite her sister offering her and then Lucy a winsome smile. The air had suddenly become sweet scented.

"It's *Eau de la vie sans souci*," Alexsis said, aware of Lucy's reaction, her lightly expanded nostrils, "in case you're wondering. Not allergic, are you? Isla pretends to be, isn't that right, sis?"

"It is potent," Isla answered. "If nothing else, it obliges the nose to pick up and take notice."

"Superior to everyday deodorant, yeah?"

"Candace recommended it for me. Says it complements my personality. We call it *Sans Souci* for short."

"Sounds Champs Élysées."

"One of Candace's associates created it. He worked for one of the big houses over there. The scent is hyacinth based, apparently, sweet, spicy, and inspirational. Candace learned that the violet hyacinth, the predominant flower in the formula, symbolizes deep regret, but believes that advertising has succeeded in turning that notion around. So, you two, reliving last night's success or reminiscing about our shared past?"

"Both," Lucy replied, taking note of how Alexsis' dazzling, watchful brown eyes seemed to fill with light, expressing a kind of glossy contentment.

"And also how successful you've become in your chosen profession, Alexsis."

"Moderately successful. Consider Isla here, looking her best in hand-me-downs that even abused manikins would reject as being in stylishly poor taste. Yes, and speaking of last night, I might have dressed the moderator Madame Belle a little differently, for someone her age, I mean."

"Please, don't tell us," Isla put in, replacing her wine glass exactly just so after taking a sip, "all that was missing were showroom feathers."

"Not likely, given the listening audience," Alexsis responded, looking slightly amused. "You see, Lucy, my lovely sister Isla celebrates an execrable taste in attire."

Isla shrugged off the tribute with a frown that gradually transformed itself into an indulgent smile that said she'd heard it all before.

Alexsis asked Islas pointedly, "The Seamstress Quick Review Friday, did Candace get the three of us tickets? Forgot to ask last night with all the fanfare."

"She did."

"You will dress up for the event. True? Not don your riches to rags like you wanted to for the readings. You know, Lucy, I had to twist her arm to put on that dress and drop the slashed jeans."

"Brilliant."

"Alexsis," Isla said, raising a finger and tapping the side of her head, "it just hit me, you could bring out something voguc-oriented in denim directed at 'with-it' teens. Call the line Misnomer Dungarees. They would fly off the shelf."

"Lucy," Alexsis said, dismissing the comment with a sweeping gesture of her right hand," I must have you visit our Excelsior State Creations. The studio is in the garment district. Midtown. Tomorrow afternoon would work for me."

"My flight home is booked. Next assignment might be the Olympics. Scheduling, yeah. So, no Seamstress Quick Review either, unfortunately."

Looking over towards the bar to where Bert stood, Isla said, "Let's order, shall we?"

On the instant, Bert appeared by the table and slid three menus smartly into place like a dealer dispensing cards at a poker game. He stood by attentively, poised.

"He also serves," Isla said, "who only stands and waits."

"Milton," Bert said in return and grinned. "Close enough." He backed away and returned to attend at the bar.

"Bring us your best bottle, Bert," Lucy called out. "Merlot, yeah? It's on me, ladies, on my expense account. I've been cutting corners on tea. Today's different."

"No need," Alexsis objected.

"I insist."

Lucy knew what she would be ordering. She found it rewarding again to observe the two siblings, occupied for the moment with perusing the menus. Alexsis Troyes, her raven-dark hair asymmetrically bobbed and her eyes brown and penetrating, and Isla Troyes, a brunette with dreamy, blue eyes and freckled, up-turned nose: they resembled each other more than they didn't, and she thought that even a Pablo Picasso in an abstract mood, his brush held out before him speculatively for the family portrait, could not mistake them for anything but sisters. An olive complexion was common to both, but where Alexsis added cosmetic touches to her cheeks, Isla refrained from doing so. Indeed, a lot like sisters but so different in character.

Lucy remembered how they were on the *Iphigenia*: Alexsis was always unconstrained except for aphasic blips where she found herself searching for the right pejorative to hang on Conrad Steele whereas Isla was generally more reserved, exhibiting a guarded manner, and was described by a fellow English guest as always keeping shtum.

"We have a plethora of choices here," Alexsis said, shaking her head slowly. "Can't figure out what to go with."

"So, don't you like anything offered here?" Isla asked.

"Of course I do, I just can't make up my mind."

"Then you should have said something like plenitude of choices, not plethora."

"Plethora means a lot of something," Alexsis explained. "You hear it used to signify an abundance. Isn't that right, Lucy?"

"Quite so. And sometimes it means a surplus, yeah?"

"Well as far as I know," Isla added, "the word plethora used to have a negative connotation. *Too much* of something as opposed to *so much* of something."

"Well, language changes, doesn't it? You, sister, of all people should know that. And your plenitude as a descriptive in the context of items available on a menu is, I'll put it this way, a bit too full of itself."

"Too clever by half, that," Isla objected. "Okay, would you deny someone saying that Candace exemplifies pulchritude."

"I would not look askance at him or her for saying so, but I think you've made your point. So, I'm going to have the tagliatelle kale pesto. I've decided."

And at this juncture Bert, smiling broadly, came over to the table with a bottle of Merlot, uncorked it, presented a short sample for Lucy to judge, which she did with approval. He poured three glasses to half-full and then proceeded to take orders. Having done so with deft and measured exactitude, he backed away from the table and disappeared.

"He's on point, isn't he?" Alexsis opined.

"A quick lad, so he is," Lucy said. "Clever, very clever. I might even call him erudite."

"To this impromptu reunion," Alexsis said, raising her glass for the others to clink, "a toast."

"Cheers."

"Yeah, the *Iphigenia* experience," Alexsis went on, having savoured a measure of wine. Her lips glistened. "Admittedly, I was little more than buzz kill for a lot of the guests. Seven days of failed conflict resolution and then that final upheaval which put everybody onboard on edge even more. A lifetime ago, seemingly."

"Can't forget that extended night in the Bruges hotel afterwards," Lucy said. "The three of us. A lot of water under those old bridges, yeah?"

"By the way, sis, I thought you did a superb job last night of reminding us how it all shook down and why."

"She was absolutely brilliant," Lucy said, tapping Alexsis appreciatively on the arm.

"I remember first seeing you getting ready to set out, Lucy. Prepping the bikes that were unloaded from the upper deck of the *Iphigenia*. You and your sidekick, whose name ..."

"Vanessa De la Croix."

"Vanessa, right. You both wore bright yellow scrunchies in your hair. You were dressed in cycling shorts and jerseys of vibrant colours, like you were part of a racing team. Could hardly tell you apart except for the difference in height."

"Vanessa has long shapely legs. Mine are shorter and more muscular."

"To tell you the truth, Alexsis described you privately at the time as shawty."

"Shawty?"

"A youngish, attractive woman," Isla explained. "It's a term of endearment, actually."

"Precisely," Alexsis asserted. "Maybe short in size but definitely large in stature. Neither frumpy nor totally with it!"

"That's me, mate, to a T. Neither nor. Still trying to distinguish the implicit from the explicit."

"Neither does shawty suggest you'd make it big on the catwalk," Alexsis went on, "nor would Vanessa be out of place there, if given the opportunity."

"I blush with coy misgiving for both of us," Lucy said, mock self-deprecation evident. She sipped some wine and laughed. "Since we're into reminiscing, I can remember seeing you for the first time, Alexsis, up on the deck of the *Iphigenia* attired entirely in black — black tights, black skirt, black blouse, black lips and black fingernails."

"As I said, buzz kill personified."

Lucy remembered that during Isla's reading of *Mourning Becomes Alexsis* last night, various recollections surfaced as to the impression Alexsis' dark clothing had elicited among other *Iphigenia* guests: the aggrieved Alexsis made a pastime of enmity; Alexsis' anguished discontent was palpable; Alexsis lived in a state of denial and bitter disbelief concerning her father's death; for Alexsis, grieving had evolved into a full-time occupation to the detriment of the whole family.

What was Geoff Cantor's observation about how other guests must have seemed during their time together on the *Iphigenia*, both participants in the drama and spectators of it? Like a classical Greek chorus full of tragic presentiment, curious about what was unfolding and yet holding back ironic observation. Close enough.

And Lucy remembered her own snide comment, "You'd think Alexsis might have had it all out with some agony aunt by now." How then could she have been epitomized in Isla's poem as Boadicea, Joan of Arc, or Medea?

"Buzz kill, maybe," Lucy said, agreeing with Alexsis' take, "but with reason, as I recall. Much came out in the conversations you and I had, even in those we had cycling along. In fact— maybe I informed you of this or maybe I didn't, I cannot be sure— I overheard Kat say to Eleni a couple of days out, 'That little bitch of a daughter, I'll strangle her one of these days.'"

"No, hadn't heard that but it's typical of things I did hear, if you catch my meaning. I'm sure I gave as good as I got although I had a time of it coming up with novel ripostes to much of Kat's antagonism. She talked *at* us more than *to* us. That covered most of our growing up years, didn't it Isla?"

"My sister is very inventive when it comes to setting the record straight. And much more the attack dog that I could ever be as you probably realized long before now. Staying silent was only so successful in assuaging feelings of inadequacy, a tactic I pretty well perfected. Occasionally I conned myself into believing lies, otherwise I tiptoed around troublesome issues and avoided reprimand."

"She was constantly apologizing for no good reasons at all."

"My release always took a different form from how Alexsis rebelled. It was more interior, more subjective. I wrote poems, Lucy. You've read them."

"I have and they have inspired me in ways I might not have anticipated. And as to those two most disturbing deaths, all of us on the *Iphigenia* were affected in one way or another. Alexsis, do you remember Geoff Cantor?"

"I do. Ball hat. Into sound editing. Son in Greece doing archaeological excavations. A nice guy. Very patient with me and my rants."

"Righto. A decent bloke and very observant. An early impression of his had you trapped in some desolate, lonely place between supplication and despair, but that particular impression of his quickly changed, I believe."

"Geoff Cantor seemed like somebody I could talk to, somebody I could trust. He was very understanding."

Mention of Geoff Cantor initiated a general wine-flavoured reminiscence about all the characters from the trip, Alexsis and Isla sliding into competitive mode to see who could remember the most about any given individual, picking up with the wry Frank Veridis from Lucy and Geoff Cantor's table in the *Iphigenia* dining area and spreading into the kitchen to include the chef's assistant. Not quite what Lucy hoped would come of their little luncheon social, with time together such a valued commodity. This was especially the case where the details of Kat's demise were uppermost on her list of events to explore further. How could she not fill in missing details and create a totally accurate picture with Alexsis now sitting next to her and in an expansive frame of mind? Lucy would make every effort to follow through on the theme that taunted her since arriving in New York City, how Kat Steele died.

"Geoff Cantor had a run-in with Conrad," Lucy stated, attempting to get back on track when Isla launched into a vivid description of the two Belgian police officers who conducted inquiries and interviewed all onboard. "Geoff told me that the particulars in his less than cordial exchange with Conrad came out in his interview with police authorities. They were pursuing every conflict onboard the *Iphigenia* that involved the murdered Conrad."

"Conrad took him to task," Alexsis recalled, "for being friendly to us and to Boyd-Alexander especially."

"I remember that scene in the lounge," Isla said. "Conrad was decked out in white chinos trousers, a silky, pale blue shirt, and around his neck a paisley cravat."

"That's showing some sense of style on your part, Sis. If only—"

"That's pretty much how you describe him in a poem," Lucy said, tapping Isla's arm.

"After cycling," Isla added, "he'd drenched himself with macho-style eau de cologne. Knock you over. Like in cartoons."

"Once their little set-to that day concluded," Lucy put in, unwilling to reduce the man's memory to mere caricature, "Geoff Cantor gave him his dues. To his way of thinking, Conrad was not a big, truculent, nasty, loud-mouthed and impatient man, a Charlton Heston character, for example, all brow and bravado and deep-throated exhortation. No, he was a smooth operator who was chief executive officer of a large corporation, an urbane, take-charge kind of guy. Generous of him, yeah?"

"Ye-aah," Alexsis said, "way too generous if he was describing the Conrad we all knew."

"Ah, at last," Isla said, watching Bert arrive with three plates, two of them balanced expertly on his left arm. She smiled at him with delight and said she was virtually starving.

Bert set each plate where it was destined to go and nodded. He backed away and returned immediately with an additional plate, a more ornate platter than the service dish, and placed it within easy reach of all three of the women. He topped up the wine glasses with a flourish. A melange of aromas wafted about the table overpowering the lingering redolence of Alexsis' *Eau de la vie San Souci.*

"Savoury dishes all around. *Bon appétit*, ladies," he said and withdrew.

"Looks very appetizing," Isla said regarding with evident delight her pesto zucchini chicken sandwich. "I'll dig in, but I'll soon have to run. Know what, this gabfest has been wonderfully entertaining. Thank you, Lucy."

"Cheers, mate," Lucy said sizing up the meatball slider sitting like a miniature tower on the plate before her. She arranged her napkin appropriately.

"The tagliatelle kale pesto looks delicious," Isla said to Alexsis, peering speculatively across the table. She then slid her knife off the table seemingly with intent, which action immediately brought Bert back with a new one held out ahead of him. He polished it on a towel he had over his arm and then handed it to her with a flourish, a knight at the service of his lady.

"Too bad I gotta go so soon," Isla said and quartered her sandwich with the newly polished knife.

"It is delicious," Alexsis managed to say after swallowing a mouthful of her pesto delight and following it with a delicate gulp of wine.

"Anyhow, discussing such matters as we are, the trip, what happened on it, and so on," Isla opined, "is like daylighting a river where, after decades of importune exploiting, what was there originally is brought back to a more natural state. That's what commentators and reporters such as you call it. Right, Lucy?"

"Righto. True enough."

"Apply the daylighting trope to our family in the correct context, Bruges, before and after, and imminent recovery— well, at least for the two of us recovery was imminent. Forrest was caught in a different set of circumstances."

"He still is."

"He's more resilient than he seems, Isla. Always was. But— "

"Would love to meet him, I would," Lucy said, looking for a purchase to that secluded and mysterious element in the family dynamics, but knowing that it was unlikely she'd succeed at this point in the discussions. "At any rate, ladies, getting back to the *Iphigenia*, do you remember the Villa Tinto incident? I was always puzzled by Kat's antics that night. Were they really a reflection of her concern for Conrad's welfare or staged to curb your intransigent behaviour?"

"Both," Alexsis said firmly. "Both."

"Before setting out for the Villa Tinto," Isla said, after slowly dabbing her lips, "Conrad sat with Kat, Boyd Alexander, and me in a rhythm and blues bar in the Grote Markt."

"I was not among them," Alexsis stated, placing her napkin on the empty plate before and pushing it slightly to the side. She reached into the central platter that Bert so artfully arranged and picked up one of the cinnamon beignets and began to nibble.

"As I remember it," Isla continued, "Conrad expected Boyd Alexander to accompany him deeper into the city 'to enhance his knowledge of the world' as he put it. Boyd Alexander protested. He was angry. Conrad insisted he was offering him a unique father-son experience. When Boyd refused absolutely, Conrad set off alone, leaving us questioning his intentions."

"His intentions were to pay for a unique experience of his own," Alexsis said. She snickered and licked her lips.

Lucy recalled that when the scene shifted to the *Iphigenia* lounge and the matter of the missing Conrad was being handled by the captain, Kat was near hysterical. Her voice billowed with angry accusation at Boyd Alexander then at Alexsis. Alexsis might have come across like some dark, romantic heroine full of doubt and disquiet; her virtually palpable sadness and obdurate resistance paled by comparison with her mother's histrionics.

Isla finished her sandwich, picked up her glass and inspected it, and then murmuring satisfaction, swallowed what red wine remained in it. She checked her phone.

After all the plates were nudged aside, Bert appeared and moved the platter of beignets from the centre of the table to a position within easy reach for Isla. He collected utensils and plates efficiently and silently and carried them off to the scullery.

"I'm pretty sure I'll be coming back to the Bistro Massimo for their delectable offerings. I'll see you around, sis. Thank you so much, Lucy. Good luck with your next assignment."

"Cheers, mate. Grand of you to come today."

"One donut good, two donuts bad," Isla said, readying herself to leave. "I'll have to pass on them. No, I'll have one."

Beignet consumed, her hands wiped clean of sugar, Isla slid out from the table. She sidled over to the bar where Bert was serving and asked directions to the ladies room. Amused, Lucy and Alexsis were watching and listening. A big smile lit up Isla's countenance when Bert pointed the way to what was obvious, given the arrow-shaped sign reading WC.

"Nice knees," Bert called out after her.

When Isla finally made it to the exit, Alexsis shook her head. Lucy could not decide if the gesture was indicative of dismay or delight. She righted her wire rim glasses that she inadvertently knocked when waving Isla out.

"She's got new confidence, that girl," Alexsis said. "But those jeans. Even the waiter had to comment."

"Right."

"Who's that, looking at me with such intellectual fervour? Your t-shirt, Lucy."

"James Joyce, the renowned Irish writer," Lucy replied, casting an eye at the blouse Alexsis was wearing.

"This? I picked it up browsing in one of Isla's thrift shops. She didn't recognize it. Obviously. You see, wearing it today was a kind of test. If you want to be on top of the next fashion craze, you have to find out what those who won't be able to afford the next fashion craze are presently wearing, then you improvise and jack up the price. I call it high-end vintage, cozying up to the cosplayers who want something not identified as bombazine."

"She'd write a poem about it, yeah? Something satirical."

"She only glanced at these," Alexsis added, drawing Lucy's attention to her earrings. These expensive silver darlings are modelled on what some local artisan fashioned from a couple of plastic plectrums, guitar most likely. Same thrift store. Costume jewelry counter. Cost of plastic originals, two dollars."

"Isla would be amused, I daresay."

"Isla's a great kid," Alexsis said. "She's determined in her own unique way to get on with things. She was totally undervalued growing up under Conrad and Kat, control freaks that they were. She was never appreciated for her innate abilities. Her low self-esteem was unwarranted, the ugly creation of self-absorbed, pseudo-loving parents. Her feeling inadequate was fabricated on totally false premises. Thankfully, success in having her poetry published has reduced its effect on her psyche. What do you think of it?"

"The poetry is good, I think. Insightful psychologically. But I'm not intellectually equipped or trained to evaluate a work to determine whether it has significant literary merit or not. I just like something I read or I don't. Simple."

"Kat would not be moved by any of it. Resentful, most likely. On the other hand, I refused to accept what Kat thought of my designs. Mediocre at best, she maintained. She'd be dismayed, overwhelmed by what I've accomplished in the last two years. Whether she'd congratulate me is another question."

"I can picture Kat relaxing on the upper deck of the *Iphigenia* taking the sun, or later at the bar, legs crossed, meticulously groomed and turned out, those glossed lips of hers shimmering with reflected light. In her right hand a cocktail, her glorious ring holding down the left hand like an emblazoned anchor."

"Sound like something Isla might have come up with."

"So, Kat's death, an overdose, yeah? Isla's poem pretty well affirms that, developing through considerable imagery what she asserted to be the crux of the matter."

"Yeah, I know the poem. I helped her with it. She was working on it in a little garden park not far from here. Corner of Sixth Avenue and Bleeker. A couple of other poems as well."

"Brilliant. And Isla told me it was suicide just like the authorities declared."

"Right. That's what she believes."

"Was Kat a closet heroin user, do you think? We never touched on such a possibility that long night of the soul in your Bruges hotel room."

"A habitual user? Don't think so. No."

"Did any of you pick up on possible symptoms of extended use on her part? Did she at any time seem unusually euphoric? That kind of thing."

"Kat, euphoric? Never!"

"Right."

"But, yes, Kat's death resulted from an overdose of heroin, no doubt about it. All was confirmed in the final medical report that Belgian officials produced for us. Typical indicators were Kat's bluish fingernails and lips."

"The bluish effect is caused by weak pulse, low blood pressure, and so it goes. Statistically, most deaths where heroin is involved are caused by loss of breathing. My knowledge of heroin addiction is limited. But I do understand that, when used, heroin gets metabolized into morphine which affects opiate receptors in the brain and that produces the so-called high."

"No, nothing like that was ever observed by either Isla or me. She only got high by abusing her children, especially Forrest."

"Ah, yes, Forrest."

"Kat was on prescription drugs. Had high blood pressure. She was secretive about her prescribed medications, too proud to admit she needed any. That might have, oh, I don't know, led to complications, given that heroin was definitely identified as influencing her death. Facts point to it being a suicide. She was drunk and virtually passed out before retiring to her berth that night. It's all behind us now, demons and all. Gone and virtually forgotten. Buried in the past."

"It seems to me that Isla exorcised her demons through the publication of a memoir. She gained control over what ailed her. Mastered it in published words. That's pretty powerful."

"Yeah, I get that completely. A kind of revenge."

"And for you, it seems that the truth has prevailed. And your rise in the fashion industry, that's pretty powerful too. Now, your brother Forrest? How has he fared?"

Alexsis assumed a look that Lucy had not seen before. The stony grin of a Sphinx caught blinking, embarrassed to have been captured shying away from the answer a passer-by gave to the challenge it posed. It was as though by inadvertently twisting a hank of her dark hair Alexsis was causing herself considerable discomfort, no, emotional pain. When she relaxed her furrowed brow and cozied into a comfortable position, she said, "I supposed we'd get around to discussing him before the afternoon was done. It's like this. Sometimes life delivers you a proposal that you cannot resist, in fact, you welcome it wholeheartedly."

"Interesting, indeed. What proposal?"

"I'll get to that all in good time. Remember, Lucy, I trusted you implicitly on the *Iphigenia,* in the Bruges hotel, and I trust you the same now."

"Of course, of course."

"Before I get to that overwhelming proposal, some further insight."

"Yes, please go on."

"I was always one with Forrest in an attempt to cross the divide that separated us from our rightful dues. More so than Isla, who was largely passive. Forrest went through periods where he roamed untethered from reality, bouncing like a red rubber ball into areas of psychic disorder."

"Right. You told me about that back on the *Iphigenia* and also in a long, elaborate email that I received from you in Paris. In it was what I thought to be speculative material to do with the way Conrad was murdered, a lead into your series of *'what if's'* that gave me much pause. There was also the gaslighting essay. I could not for the life of me bring those two documents up on my computer. Buried password, yeah?"

"Yes, I remember sending the emails to you. Passwords can be a pain."

"At that time I thought if I pursued the point, you'd just brush off all the *what if's* as pure fantasy after you'd endured a traumatic experience— the way Isla might compose a poem steeped in emotional self-revelation."

"As I said, it's all behind us now. Well, for Isla and me it is." Alexsis' voice, tense and tremulous moments before when describing Conrad's hold on them, grew softer, became more soothing in effect as sensitive understanding replaced what had sounded so negative. She went on. "Sadly, Forrest still wrestles with troubling memories. It's like he's suffered from a life-long curse. As to what happened on the *Iphigenia*, the real story never came out except for what happened to Dolf Van Handelaar."

"Didn't he claim in his defense that some American tourist played him?"

"So I heard."

"I know about being stitched up," Lucy said, tapping a finger on the table.

"Stitched up?"

"Set up. Conned. Framed."

"For what? Writing some article about corruption, social inequity, or saving the environment? Who?"

"The authorities. Sod the bent ones among them! Or those toffs in a position to thwart my efforts to speak truth to power. Got fobbed off on lesser issues, not that rescuing the environment is not important. Played it low-key for a stint after the threats. All bullocks."

"Threats? What kind of threats?"

"Threats that upset my equilibrium, verbal, written, social media trolling, and the like. Even physical threats. Got questioned by coppers in rumpled suits down at the nick. Have a record on form, available to authorities influenced by corrupt politicians. Civil cases raised their ire. The ugly profiles of Russian oligarchs came out of the shadows. The scar-face of organized crime seemed less threatening."

"So, you were actually set up, Lucy. By comparison, Dolf Van Handelaar got it easy although he didn't get off."

"Likely. I always thought there was more to his story, especially where Kat comes in, or more accurately, where Kat goes out. How it happened seemed too cut and dried. I, like most people at one time or another, indulge in speculation, but a lot of the time my hunches prove revealing, especially given my full-time occupation as an investigative reporter."

"Precisely."

At this juncture Lucy knew, judging by Alexsis' demeanour and guarded assertions, that she had the purchase she'd been seeking. All she had to do was coax Alexsis with encouraging words and kindly murmurs which, ironically, Alexsis seemed not to need in telling all that she knew. As it turned out, all that she knew was all that mattered. It was everything, the whole truth.

"How about an Irish coffee?" Lucy offered and Alexsis accepted the offer.

Chapter 14
Eureka

Let it be understood at this juncture that the propagation of truth and the promulgation of prophecy, as I outlined above, are not my only divinely sanctioned mandates. As well as being the god of light in all its manifestations — intellect, reason, knowledge, understanding, sunshine, to say nothing of my responsibilities regarding the establishment of urban centres, the maintenance of civil order, and the administration of justice (of which I will have much to say forthwith)— my directorship, as Isla Troyes pointed out more than once and I deem necessary to repeat here, my directorship covers the wide world of inspiration, afflatus, which denotes, the well-informed know, divine impulse. Hence further enlightenment, such being in no way a contradiction to my earlier declared disinclination to ramble. Behold Homer, Sophocles, Aurelius, Virgil, Dante, Leonardo, Shakespeare, Milton, Mozart, Shelley, Jefferson, Dumas, Dostoyevsky, Baudelaire, Joyce, Chopin, Sartre, Picasso,

Mann, a mere random selection of creative geniuses in the arts, in music, in philosophy, and in politics. Louis XIV, the would-be *roi soleil*, was an aberration, a walking, talking, fornicating and defecating oxymoron. Moving on: with my input, Archimedes, Copernicus, Newton, and Einstein advanced human understanding of the physical world and the earth's place in the universe. Aristophanes, Molière, Monty Python presented generic truth in the farcical forms that I inspired. Benny Hill, Peter Sellers, and Milton Berl, cavorting good humorously under my aegis, also rate well in the world of comedic entertainment. And let not the wordsmith of satirical commentary George Carlin be forgotten. In the interest of what enhances Lucy's appreciation of time spent in Greenwich Village, it should be taken for granted that I influenced Edward Hooper's singular use of light in his compositions: I fired up his inner artist.

In a more modest application of my powers, I have urged a struggling painter to adopt a new palette, a mediocre student to compose a brilliant essay, an MD in research to scratch his head and then cry, Eureka! I refrain from proclaiming the possibilities that AI proposes because as of yet I have not been granted the key to the universal algorithm but, I prophesize, that day and that gift are coming soon. I refrain from commenting on biological and cyborg engineering as I have no real redundancy in these fields of twenty-first century research, although I have inspired futurists to consider all possibilities regarding human destiny. However, I will venture to nod approvingly at evolutionary psychology which teaches that a long-established need to be in touch with the transcendental source of beauty and truth, which exists beyond the structures of animism, continues even if considered subjectively superfluous to peace of mind. In the meantime, be impressed at least with how I encouraged the master builders and guild workers who erected the Gothic cathedrals; given the limitations of the medieval world, these monuments dedicated to a higher order are architectural wonders that have endured the tests of time.

Ancients initially thought that we gods and goddesses first made ourselves known in the minds of mortals through their dreams. True. Nietzsche referred to me as the master of illusion, an accurate evaluation and a welcome compliment. Diverse theories, the work of psychologists like Jung, evolved: these enhanced our standing, and rightfully so. Inspired individuals, engaged in contemporary conversations, will declare that a brilliant idea came to light when an electric bulb flashed on. Only a lightning strike would improve that metaphor.

Rumours over the centuries have lauded Dionysus as a source of creative energy equal to mine. Let me put the record straight: mine is a full-time occupation while his is, and always has been, part-time and entirely dependent on squeezing and stomping the grape. I leave the controversy to learned philosophers, impartial literary critics, and reviewers operating beyond a simplistic and formulaic frame of mind.

As to immediate instances of my illustrious raison d'être, I declare it is I who prompted Lucy Hunter to seek truth unstintingly. Even voguish Alexsis Troyes has succeeded in her extravagant designs in light of my airy intimations. Her extravagant actions on the *Iphigenia,* however, lay outside my direct influence. She has yet to reveal much to Lucy and, I sense, she is readying herself to do so. What came about under the circumstances that Lucy is attempting to understand completely, came about under the blanket of darkness.

In keeping with my avowed Delphic inducement to *Know Thyself*, let me declare the following: regarding her stint on the *Iphigenia,* Alexsis Troyes knew herself for what she was and for what she knew herself capable of. Hubris did not bring her down. No enraged Furies pursued her. The point is, I am not guiltless of transgression and therefore I cast no aspersions. What concerns her brother is another question entirely, one soon to be understood more thoroughly by Lucy Hunter and anyone following her inquiries. My impetus, of course.

Before returning to Lucy and Alexsis, it is incumbent upon me to disclose my own iniquity. In the service of absolute truth, that is. Some commentators have labelled it unrighteous and totally contradictory in the ultimate illuminator, me. But, like all the Olympians, I reflect the human propensity to harm those who offend. I, too, fought primitive urges and then upon reflection and the infusion of celestial grace allowed benign light to supplant those urges. Nonetheless, I do accept those legitimate charges lodged against me, complaints known in contemporary parlance as dirty tricks.

The Trojan priestess Cassandra comes immediately to mind. The gift of prophecy I bestowed on her as incentive to an imminent and dynamic amorous attachment, I twisted into a perversion of truthful soothsaying when she refused my immediate advances. Because of the curse I laid on her, she would never be trusted as capable of actually foretelling the future. None believed her warnings, the Trojans in particular. This requital on my part was self-serving and illustrated the abuse of power. I was guilty of disregarding my own dictum, *nothing in excess.* There were other instances where I indulged in nasty reprimands and reprisal but I let the sad story of Cassandra at this juncture in the unfolding narrative stand for all.

Consider Lucy Hunter's position. I am not forwarding any sort of prophecy here, just a modest prediction given her predilection to uncover all the salient facts, to hypothesize in the service and declaration of truth as she understands it. Eventually, she, too, will have to choose. The present hiatus from dialogue directed at disclosure concludes here. Enough discourse. Irish coffee is in the offing, not that discourse and Irish coffee are incompatible.

Remarkably, Lucy found herself in what she would term liminal space, the peripheral position betwixt and between, balancing active inquisitiveness and passive acceptance. She imagined emerging from a species of dream state that engrossed her while Alexsis absented herself to take a call. Surreal. It came over her, she figured, by watching a moth circling around the elegant bistro chandelier. That sense of unreality experienced upon waking passed quickly enough, allowing her to slide out of the domain of mythic archetypes back to the quotidian.

Chapter 15
Emblazoned Phoenix

Back in her booth in the Bistro Massimo, Lucy entertained the doubt that the pique of conscience prompted Alexsis to reveal as much as she did in an email. Was her intention in sending it an effort to unburden herself of feelings of guilt? Daughter expressed no regret about mother's suicide. Uncanny, even for Alexsis. The email, as far as Lucy could remember, and remembrance of it remained vague, was nothing but a playful demonstration of Alexsis' resolve to eradicate Conrad Steele's dominance. When first read, Lucy thought of it as more of an apologia, a reasoned justification for feeling so little about the loss of Kat, and at the same time a symbolic sentencing for maternal malfeasance. If queried, Alexsis could claim total fabrication, call what she sent across nothing but imagined wish-fulfilment, a *what-if* fantasy concocted up out of having too much time on her hands before flying back to America. Whatever the case, the trust was mutual between Lucy Hunter and Alexsis Troyes and had been from the outset.

Unalloyed details, that was what she wanted most from Alexsis and that was pretty much what she got, aided and abetted by the seductive smack of the Irish coffee.

Alexsis' detailed narrative led back to the demise of Victor Troyes and included two of the *what ifs* that Lucy had been harping on. What if Kat never forgave Victor for sacrificing their daughter, Jennifer, and believed he deserved to die for his egotistical miscalculation? Alexsis remembered Kat in a rage heaping aspersions on her cursed husband and accusing him of filicide, of sacrificing their beloved daughter to his vast ego. Alexsis confirmed that she and Forrest suspected early that Kat and Conrad Steele conspired in their amorous liaison to have Victor taken out by professionals. Same with Casandra Fortune. Despite protests, Forrest and Alexsis were denied attendance at her funeral. In no way, despite their limited understanding of the world at that stage in their lives, could they be convinced that Cassie was a junkie. Arguing the point, they were again put in their place. When Alexsis informed Virgil Troyes, their uncle, of what they thought about both deaths, the first being a murder, and the second being so confusing and yet connected to the first in ways they could not adequately explain, he assured them that in the end the truth would out. The convictions that she and Forrest held would never falter.

Once Conrad had established himself as master of the household by marrying Kat, life for Forrest, Alexsis, and Isla became intolerable. Eventually Alexsis wrote her treatise on gaslighting, a psychological and emotional mechanism by which they were tricked into accepting lies as truth. Lucy was cognizant of some details of the emotionally impoverished existence the three children had to suffer as a result of the parental brainwashing. And yet, Alexsis emphasized, she and Forrest persisted in their rebellious noncompliance. She indeed revelled, as she heard Isla proclaim in one conversation on the *Iphigenia*, in something like an ecstasy of hate for both Conrad and Kat. Her misery on display, she engaged in more than just passive-aggressive behaviour toward them, it was out and out attack mode.

Conrad's response to Forrest, the more aggressive of the two intransigents, was to declare unequivocally that Forrest was a lost cause, that he was not "all there" because as a child he suffered a fall and seriously injured his brain. He insisted with cynical certitude that complete madness lay in Forrest's future. Truth is, a force-field of conflict had enveloped the two of them; in other words, Alexsis explained, Conrad suspected that Forrest was on to him. With Kat's acquiescence, Conrad further claimed that Forrest suffered from incipient madness, quoting school reports of distracted and aggressive behaviours that confirmed what doctors had determined to be the cause of Forrest's troubles, Post Traumatic Stress Disorder.

Granted, Alexsis affirmed, Forrest was significantly aggrieved by the death of his father and resented Conrad replacing him. Victor treated Forrest like the dauphin, the heir apparent. In time that would equate to head of the company and a whole lot more. Conrad had his own successor in Boyd Alexander who had yet to prove his tanist capabilities, and so the continued bickering of the father-son conflict. Alexsis understood that. She also understood all too well how vindictive Conrad could be. Lucy already knew a great deal of what Alexsis was divulging but hearing her repeat it all was a definite sign there was more, a lot more, to come. Alexsis continued her account by covering as many of the *what if's* she could in retrospect recall. She even added to them.

What if, Conrad Steele's assailant that last night on the *Iphigenia* were Forrest Troyes seeking retribution? What if, Flex and Alexis witnessed the dumping of the body but only reported seeing a hoodie guy on a cargo bike rushing away from the scene of the crime? What if, Forrest procured heroin from Van Handelaar with a very specific reason in mind? What if, actions taken by Forrest and his accomplices led to the brutal elimination of Conrad Steele? What if, phone messages provided evidence of a conspiracy between brother and sister to commit serious crimes? What if, a distressed and inebriated Kat were sedated by a daughter who then aided in administering a lethal dose of heroin? What if, that daughter was not Isla?

These hypothetical questions that Alexsis unloaded almost by rote prompted Lucy to think back to the protracted discussion she and Isla and Alexsis had in the Bruges hotel on the night of Kat's demise. When they called it a night and all feverous regret had been expressed to the point of exhaustion, Lucy had wondered: could it be that Alexsis had simply been hiding behind her outward grievances, her rejected daughter discontent, her sardonic jabs, and was she just waiting for the propitious moment? And what if, by including the *what if's* in her email, she were simply working out possibilities as to how events might have been interpreted had authorities pursued events to the fullest. Once Alexsis opened up to the extent that she had, Lucy did not want to accuse herself of gaining vital info from the slow drip of innuendo, a phrase the sardonic Frank Veridis had come up with. She sought only statements of fact.

"When viewing at close range," Alexsis continued after a moment's hesitation in which she slid the empty coffee cup towards the side of the table, "Conrad's heaped-up corpse after it was pulled from the canal, the fury that lay hidden within for so long burst forth and I willingly embraced the cruel act I knew I, in theory, was capable of. I knew absolutely, as Forrest had proclaimed with Flex in agreement, that blood will have blood."

"Right, go on."

"Once Forrest and Flex were committed to their parts, I could not neglect to do mine."

"So, matricide. Sedation and lethal injection, antidotes to years of grievance, yeah?" Lucy spooned the creamy remnants of her coffee, smacked her lips after ingesting it, and repositioned her spoon as though it were capable of pointing to what Alexsis would say next.

"Absolutely, years of grievance. In her poem, Isla phrased it in similar language. We kept her out of it. She's still totally in the dark as to our involvement. She retained her innocence, but in her memoir she remembered and articulated well the agony she suffered in silence."

"That leaves me wondering about the fate of one Dolf Van Handelaar. No CCTV coverage of the area, as far as we know?"

"None."

Alexsis hesitated then slid the emptied coffee cup to the side as though clearing space for her response to Lucy's double-edged prompt. What if Dolf Van Handelaar really was set up by a young American as he claimed when arrested by Belgian police? Forrest was in Belgium,

Alexsis said, during the later part of *Iphigenia* adventure. He entered and left the country under a false identity, calling himself Richard Boone. His passport was fake, a very good fake. He and Flex arrived together in Antwerp at the same time and had reservations on the same flight home from Brussels.

Forrest connected with Dolf Van Handelaar through a friend here in Brooklyn who had spent some time in Amsterdam and who had some goods on Dolf. Leverage, by another name. As pre-arranged, Forrest met Van Handelaar in Antwerp and set about effecting their devious stratagem, total retribution its goal. Dolf had no choice but to buy into the scheme. For his part, Forrest followed the route of the *Iphigenia* surreptitiously, communicating with Flex and Alexsis only when necessary. In his role as facilitator, Dolf Van Handelaar followed the route more openly.

Lucy remembered that aside from being of assistance to Isla and Candace, the hooded Dolf had been sighted several times in Bruges, notably communicating with Flex down in the bike parkade below Sint-Michielsbrug and again pushing his cargo bike among the tourists across the bridge itself. The sightings raised interest at the time but no concern at all.

That aforementioned "irresistible and welcomed proposal" was presented to Alexsis the very night that Flex arrived on the *Iphigenia*. He was more than a friend in the guise of messenger. This was exactly what happened, Alexsis avowed to Lucy listening intently, because she was there and a willing party to it.

When Conrad left the Bruges hotel after his business dinner with Calvin Kinlaw, he was inebriated. Weaving his way back late at night through the wooded walkway to the *Iphigenia*, he was surprized by Flex, suddenly approaching him from behind a tree. Actually, Flex accosted him. Too drunk to offer substantial resistance, Conrad lost his balance and stumbled just as Forrest appeared and delivered a lethal smack to the back of his head with a metal pipe. The blow felled Conrad Steele. Permanently. A severed finger of the left hand rendered up the prized ring. Two coins were quickly inserted into a pocket of his jacket. His body was then hefted into the cargo bin of Dolf Van Handelaar's bike. He pedaled his load across the red bridge and on to the Bargeweg. Forrest, Flex, and Alexsis all helped Dolf slide the carcass into the canal at the rear of the *Iphigenia*. Flex tossed the cork top from the phoenix jug into the murky waters. And so it was done.

The voice of dispassionate avowal, Alexsis was not teasing out the truth, or just sort of putting it out there as a possibility for her willing listener. Lucy Hunter was not a wide-eyed conspiracy theorist open to having wacky notions confirmed. It was not a pseudo confession with Alexsis coyly saying but not saying. No, she readily declared her complicity in treachery and admitted having no compunction whatsoever about it. No tears. No guilt. No regret. No sense of imminent madness about to consume her. For her, action produced consequences. All fine, and her equilibrium was not tottering in the slightest and her rightful place in the world was not threatened. Fortunate consequences of her action.

"What's done cannot be undone," Lucy commented when Alexsis stopped to catch her breath. "Conrad's severed finger? The ring? And the coins? How do these things figure in the story?"

"The ring was symbolic. In Forrest's mind, it equated to how Conrad weaseled into our lives by marrying our mother. It was a long lasting resentment, as long as mine, only more intense, more severe in its definition and, let's say, its orientation. He was determined to sever the connection, not just symbolically, but in real terms. So, off with the finger."

"The two coins?"

"A tip for the ferryman. Further symbolism."

Lucy wondered, then asked: "What if all that you divulged is the truth and nothing but? Why did you and Forrest with the aid of Flex take so long to do in Conrad? Why on a cycling adventure in Holland and Belgium?"

Donning a Cheshire cat grin, Alexsis replied: "Family circumstances outside of the ordinary where control of me was much looser. Forrest was operating behind the scene, like I've told you. As to when and where, opportunity, convenience, and a fall guy. You're well aware of our motivation, well, primarily mine and Forrest's, especially his."

"Very much so."

"We had other opportunities after Flex arrived, like the night Conrad visited the red-light area in Antwerp, the Villa Tinto. There was just too much streetlight, too many people out and around. The Bargeweg in Bruges late at night was the last chance and the best one. We took it."

"Roger that. So, if all you've said is accurate, Dolf Van Handelaar was a cut-out for Forrest and was cleverly stitched up to take the fall because of an anonymous tip to the cops that they acted on, and which led to the bloke's arrest."

"That's how Forrest planned it. With Flex's help. And I was willingly conscripted to play my part."

Lucy remembered conversing with Conrad on one of the cycling stops in Holland when, in defence of his seemingly authoritarian reaction to what was going on with Alexsis, he said that she was quite capable of lying. Was she lying now? If so, why? Lucy decided to pursue one last point, hoping to establish absolute consistency about what seemed to be cold, calculated come-uppance for wrongs committed against children.

"Right, so that's how they planned it. What about Kat? And what happened with the jug?"

"As is obvious now, Forrest was on the scene for a bit. He saw the jug at the Kunst Woestijn museum and had Flex present it to Kat. The phoenix engraving was what really grabbed Forrest's attention in addition to its colour and odd shape. So, indicative of a new beginning for us with its emblazoned phoenix, symbolic of transformation. He envisaged the jug as a vessel to contain Kat's ashes, but it went missing. Ironically, Conrad had called it a funeral urn."

Lucy considered Alexsis' explanation and nodded tentatively. She recalled that Kat despised the jug and that Conrad did call it a funeral urn when Flex presented it to her at the dinner table.

"When called into the scene of Kat's supine body on the bunk, arm hanging down, pinpoint pupils in her unshut eyes—suicide as authorities presumed—I saw the jug standing upright on Kat's valise as though it were placed exactly there as a kind of sign saying 'have a nice trip.' Mother believed in the afterlife. It struck me at that moment as kind of funny, you know, amusing."

"Righto. That's what you said to me. I was lurking about the passageway at the bottom of the stairs wondering what the devil was going on. I'd heard Isla's piercing scream."

"Cops said that the jug would be dusted for fingerprints. That never happened though."

"Logical, the dusting. And so was deciding the scene and all the evidence as pointing to suicide. But it wasn't, was it?"

"No, it was not. It was retribution," Alexsis declared with absolute clarity. After a moment's hesitation, she asked, "Not secretly recording anything here, are you, my dear? No intention of having me go so far as to begin atoning for my sins. When it comes to Kat and Conrad, I will remain unatoned for the rest of my life."

"Absolutely not," Lucy replied, shifting uneasily, trying to comport herself to respond above suspicion, to convince Alexsis that she would keep shtum. "That would be a gross betrayal. Your trust in my discretion is and always has been well placed."

"Perfect," Alexsis concluded. "Now direct me to the ladies room."

"To the right there, follow the sign," Lucy answered, believing that Alexsis' plaintive note of worried surmise might actually reveal true concern about fidelity of friendship. "Same route Isla took."

"Of course," Alexsis said, amused. She slid easily out of her seat. "Know what I would like to do, walk with you through the area. I still have an hour or so of—" Alexsis hesitated, giving into a sardonic grin, "of freedom. I have an interview with an AI rep later. We can continue talking about old times and anything else that strikes our fancy."

Lucy promptly agreed. Before Alexsis returned, she'd paid the bill, leaving Bert a handsome tip. She was completely taken aback when she just missed colliding into the broad-shouldered man with craggy face and rifled hair and sleeves of discoloured tattoos that had barged into 4TO Books ahead of her the previous night, the middle aged porn star of her precipitous denigration. He quickly looked about the bistro, an unlit matchstick rotating on his lips. Bert greeted him, shook his hand, and then accompanied him to a seat at the bar where they engaged in friendly banter. Lucy shook her head, nonplussed by what she had just witnessed. As she followed Alexsis out of the bistro, she glanced back to the conversation taking place at the bar and inadvertently dropped her daypack.

"Sod it!"

Chapter 16
No Love Lost

Even though she was keeping company with an up-and-coming maven of fashion, Lucy was glad she'd decided on shorts for the occasion. The day had warmed up considerably, but it was not overbearing. Simply stated, it was summer in the city.

At the corner of Carmine and Bleeker, Alexsis suggested, "We can mosey along to the east a little and then head up to Washington Square Park. How does that sound?"

"Super. Great area. Love these bosky Village areas."

"Bosky?"

"All the trees. Best of two worlds. Urban routes countrified."

"You don't really need a car in New York City," Alexsis said, putting on the sunglasses she took out of her purse, "even though one-way streets make for easier getting around. Like this one. And bikes are everywhere. Like right here. With taxis, they're everywhere. My favourite mode of transportation these days."

Lucy remembered that Alexsis had been a fairly competent cyclist when on the *Iphigenia* adventure. Pointing to the stalls along the Carmine Street bike path, she said, "I thought earlier of renting a Citi bike and exploring further afield. I was sitting in the square there and decided I needed a break from reading Isla's memoir and a break from all my suppositions. The water spilling over the rings of the fountain put me in mind of gurgling strings of pearls. The pigeons at my feet began mocking me. Working up a little perspiration has its rewards, so I've been told, but I doubt the wisdom in that proposition. I kept on with the reading and the suppositions. Besides, I'd forgotten my clip-on visors, good against the blaring sun."

Our Lady of Pompei church stood wide and solidly dignified cater-corner to Father Demo Square, its triple tiered steeple reaching toward the heavens like geometric building blocks piled one on top of the other. Further along Bleeker, Alexsis pointed to an apartment building several stories high, to the stark black fire escapes secured in abstract arrangement against the faded red brick. Sunlight caught the top two stories of the building. She called it serialized architectural art, New York style.

"Know what the artist Edward Hopper proclaimed about that kind of scene? That he had a sense of elation about sunlight on the upper part of a house."

"A fan, are you?"

"He's brilliant.

Lucy pointed to a woman sunbathing on the third level of the fire escape, book open on her lap.

"It's like she just emerged from Hopper's *Morning Sun* to be caged in solitude. When walking about this area of New York, which I have done on previous visits, I like looking for correspondences in the concrete world of the streets and the buildings with remembered Hopper images. I don't have all the critical language to describe my response to his work. I just liked what I saw when first exposed to it in an art appreciation course at uni. The best I can do is say it's the impressions of a realist revealing an inner life."

"You are a fan, just like our father was. He owned a landscape by Edward Hooper that I'd sit and stare at when younger. It kept me spellbound and that really bugged Conrad. Later, of course. He took it to auction. Didn't want any mementos of Father around the house."

"So you're a fan too."

"I am but what I am not a fan of is graffiti."

"Some call it urban art."

"Call it what you will, I find it off-putting."

Graffiti marring building walls and city structures put Lucy off as well, no matter the city she visited. Supersized graffiti put her off even more. Little offense so far, she was pleased to note, as they advanced along Bleecker.

"Winston Churchill Square across there is a small garden enclave. That's where Isla had me meet her, like I said earlier."

"Right. *Furies To Juries*."

A rushing cyclist cut the two women off as they made their way through the crosswalk at Sixth Avenue. Alexsis cried "Asshole" and Lucy echoed with "Wanker." They held up momentarily at the corner, then set off again.

Lucy had taken note of just how graceful Alexsis comported herself. She walked confidently, sure footed even in sandals.

"Alexsis, you seem to float along while I must hustle to keep up."

"Isla called me an archetypical sidewalk swan. She didn't mean a word of it. I think she just liked the sound of the words."

When they heard boogie-woogie piano pounding out of Little Red Square across the street, they automatically got caught up in it— the steady rhythmic base and the riffs from the upper reaches of the keys inspired unanticipated free, spontaneous foot movement. They danced along for half a block improvising steps in keeping with the music, each in her own way. Lucy dropped her bouncing daypack several times and Alexsis her purse twice and sunglasses once.

Further along Bleeker, they passed several small-scale commercial enterprises with names like Posh Pop and Pop Up and Puerto Rico and Italiano.

"So, as in Isla's poem,' Lucy prompted when the boogie-woogie had receded out of range and her keenness to get back on track took hold again, "the one you helped her with, *Furies To Juries*, your brother felt duty bound to avenge his father's murder."

Alexsis stopped momentarily to consider. "That's correct," she said and picked up again the natural rhythm her gait had established, which, aside from being graceful, was determined but not rushed. "We turn here, Lucy, on MacDougal. Watch your step."

Lucy watched her step and kept on. They walked in silence for a few hundred paces, meandering through the many passers-by, some singular, some in pairs, some in small groups. They came to a halt in front of the Grisly Pear when sounds of delight from across the street distracted them. Several cyclists, panniers loaded, coasted down the high visibility bike path, bells ringing. Stopping this way to watch reminded Lucy of her time together with Alexsis when members of a Dutch or Belgian cycling club went whistling by on racing bikes or when a respite was called for and their own pedaling stopped, and a coffee break in some quaint Lowlands town was in the offing.

They proceeded further up MacDougal and when passing the Comedy Cellar, Lucy said, "I'd thought to have taken in some smart aleck tosser in one of these clubs, but Isla's reading took precedence once I found out about it."

Alexsis' phone went off, ringing with a traditional phone sound. There was nothing exotic or fanciful about it, which pleased Lucy, whose own phone sounded just like a phone ringing when it rang. She loved debating the issue with peers. On one occasion she employed a fanciful analogy to make a point about a simple ringtone: the bas-relief of everyday communication was preferable to the high relief of exaggerated self-identification. She wasn't taken seriously.

Checking her phone, Alexsis said she had to take the call and backed into the protection of the Café Wha doorway out of the flow of pedestrians toing and froing. While Alexsis was on the phone, Lucy took the time to appreciate just where she was. Ethnic eateries of every description, streetside patios, beverage houses, cafés, music and comedy venues, a potpourri of endless possibilities set in solid scenes of varied textures and hues of brick and mortar. The thought occurred to her that anyone living in the vicinity, but most likely students attending NYU, would not go hungry or be starved for entertainment.

Add into the scene of daily commerce the surround sound of the street, swelling and then subsiding—claxons, bicycle bells, revving motors, conversations heard in passing, ambient noises, and "Ware the road" warnings from delivery men pushing squealing dollies. And add further a melange of culinary odours and flavours offering the whetted olfactory sense a challenge: how to distinguish what was redolent of elsewhere and what your nose tickled your fancy with from right here on the street. Greek, Italian, Levantine, and so much more, including Tex Mex. For Lucy, being on MacDougal at this time equated to being on any busy street in any busy city but this was New York City. She was witnessing and loving yet again the quotidian activity of stimulating Village life.

"The AI guy," Alexsis said, tapping the gawking Lucy on the shoulder. "We've another short distance to the park."

They crossed West Third Street and proceeded up the block. On their right stood Vanderbilt Hall, ivy clinging to the red brick like tenacious students with something to prove. It was like a solid construct of prose, in the literary imagination of her own making that Lucy occasionally wandered into, interspersed with figurative touches, topped with a parapet of decorative but purposeful purple prose. Desist, she told herself.

At the corner of West Fourth Street was The Center on Civil Justice At NYU

School Of Law. The sign triggered in Lucy the need to get back on topic. Sauntering along MacDougal this way was entertaining and revealing but it was not, with such a variety of distractions, very conducive to purpose. After passing Hayden Hall and its flapping flags—burning torches casting light— Alexsis pointed across to the Washington Place entrance. They followed a man leading a dog into the park. Ubiquitous greenery from shade trees and shrubbery hemmed in the walkway they followed. Familiar territory.

As they proceeded towards the central fountain, Lucy felt that a change in ambient influences was imminent. She wondered if Alexsis' phone call was important enough to have her leave before she'd provided all the information she had to share about Forrest. Turning, she gave Alexsis an inquisitive look.

"How's our time?"

"Fine, but I have to get back to the office by four-thirty at the latest. I'll hail a taxi. This AI guru wants to discuss algorithms that recognize emerging fashion trends."

"Right. Right. AI."

"You know, I could spend all day here people watching. The dog runs are a riot. Canine central. It's a very historical area. We came here as kids with Father. We had much to learn, he said."

"My hotel is just over there on Beverly Place. When in New York, I try to establish myself in this area. Edward Hopper stomping grounds, yeah? I also enjoy watching the chess players. How moves are planned ahead always intrigued me about the game."

"Do you play?"

"Not well."

"Father taught us. Forrest proved to be the best at it. Isla prevails at scrabble. She can throw words around like 'panegyric' without much hesitation. I struggled with 'vociferous' but I get it now."

"Right, panegyric and vociferous. One does not get to use them very often in ordinary conversation."

"Did you know, they do scrabble competitions here in the park?"

"Yes, I did know that," Lucy said nodding agreement and then stopping, Alexsis with her. "Getting back to what we were discussing before, I have a fairly good understanding of what motivated you in your actions. I refer to what happened in Bruges. Forrest remains a mystery other than for what you've imparted to me so far about how he actually got his hands dirty."

They began walking again.

"He and I shared so much in the early years. I've explained a lot of that already, haven't I?"

"You have, yes."

"And I see a lot of him these days. Since...well, you know..."

"Since?"

"Okay," Alexsis said firmly. She pointed to a bench, one of many surrounding the fountain. Close by on another bench sat a man wearing a straw hat, a smile on his face as wide as the ragged brim. His legs, up to the shins seemingly, were deep in jostling pigeons. Lucy waved at the man with his entourage of cooing cronies and then turned back to Alexsis.

"Let's sit here for a bit," Alexsis said, whisking a leaf off the bench.

"Perfect."

"Okay, Forrest drove himself around the bend over our so-called family situation right from the start. I just abided my time while complaining continuously and, might I add, vociferously. I suffer little now as a consequence of our —what do they call it— dastardly deed. Ours was a two-fold dastardly deed. In fact, I suffer not at all. Not so with my poor brother. I'll give you all I can, and there's a lot to give."

"Yes, of course," Lucy said agreeably. She detected a change in the cadence of Alexsis' speech. She seemed in a hurry to get the facts out but not harried about taking so much time to do so. She was pacing herself. That flinty edge in her responses from earlier was replaced with nuanced calm.

"Forrest was eventually cast in the role of prodigal son but not by choice, and he never returned to any welcoming feast or regain his rightful place in the family and, in so doing, bank his inheritance. No, none of that until Kat cashed in her chips and Conrad, well, before her."

"I follow."

"When Father died, something in Forrest died and was reborn in a kind of obsessive hate. The mother and son bond was severed. As it turned out, permanently. Kat didn't know it right off, but Forrest did, although it didn't take her too long to sense something was off, really off. I underwent a similar transition but not as severe as what Forest experienced. I didn't quite drive myself crazy. Moral outrage in a kid is hard to get your mind around especially when you're a kid yourself. At bottom, Lucy, there's a lot to take in if the truth is to be understood for what it is in its entirety. I'm sure you'll agree. Then there's the whole madness thing with Forrest, but I will get down to that."

"I have only a vague picture of what Forrest looks like. In my mind it's a kind of composite of features you and Isla share. But I really have no idea."

"Okay, no problem," Alexsis said. She reached into her purse, searched around, and pulled out a duo of photographs. "This is what Father looked like when we were kids. This is Forrest at about the time he was forced out of the house. Isla always maintained Forrest looks like a younger

196

Mark Wahlberg here, but I don't see it. I'm sentimental about both pictures."

Lucy studied the two photographs and concluded that Forrest was definitely his father's son— the brow, the broad smile, the curly locks. Mark Wahlberg, not so much.

"Righto," Lucy said, returning the photographs to Alexsis who slid them back into her purse. "I've got at least an inkling of what he might look like today. So moral outrage and madness, yeah?"

Alexsis did get right down to it and began to unravel the skein of secrecy (Lucy' term) that protected her beloved Forrest. His being mistreated in his youth to the point of abject misery combined with his absolute certainty that Conrad and Kat had his father murdered served to form a basis for revenge. This dual combination of what he considered factual did not, however, account for how deeply he suffered and the madness he endured prior to the execution of his plan and suffered more intensely subsequent to the execution of that plan.

Forrest, Alexsis, and Isla were young when their father Victor Troyes died. Kat married Conrad way too soon after she scattered a shovel full of dirt on her deceased husband's grave in a gesture considered, in Alexsis' view, a little too nonchalant. The red roses sincere mourners had placed on the casket got knocked about indifferently this way and that.

As they got older and started asking logical questions, that's when deceit and overwhelming parental supervision ("tough love bullshit" in Alexsis' exact words) came on strong, denying the three of them basic freedoms.

"As Isla wrote in her cahier—it was memorable for me— 'like dark shadows and black clouds leaching the colour out of springtime flowers, so had Conrad Steele robbed the spontaneity out of the life our father had promised us.' Something like that, anyway."

"So, no love lost."

"Ye-aah," Alexsis said, emphasizing what would be obvious to anyone who'd been listening.

"Righto," Lucy said, amused at Alexsis' elongation into two syllables a word the ear normally heard as one.

"To borrow from the infantilizing patois out there these days, I never thought of myself as a daddy's girl after my real father was killed and Forrest was never ever a momma's boy."

Alexsis looked away, focusing on the splayed white discharge of water with which the fountain was dousing the day. Noisy kids splashed about on the periphery, where side jets added to the aquatic display and to the evident fun.

After watching the frolicking for a few wistful moments, with Lucy looking on beside her, Alexsis continued her factual account of life before Bruges. Lucy remained enthralled.

Kat and Conrad contrived through gaslighting to distort memories of being with their father, their outings with him in the city and music recitals in Central Park, the family vacations, the trips to Greece. Misremembering and doubt entered their recollections. Victims of gaslighting, Alexsis contended, had to endure anxiety, depression, self-loathing, addiction, and suicidal impulses. In a word, darkness, there being many versions of darkness and many depths of depression, but there was only one brother.

The brainwashing continued. Bipolar disorder eventually supplanted PTSD as the affliction of choice in Conrad's lexicon. Given her limitations at the time, Alexsis did manage to research the concept of manic depression and its varied manifestations. Everything Conrad stated about the disorder was accurate, she concluded, only it did not apply to the brother that she knew. No way did he exhibit dramatic mood changes in any excessive way. Forrest was energetic, climbed trees, played ball, got to engage in all the usual activities a boy can get into regardless of the heavy atmosphere endured in the company of Kat and Conrad. He was never the so-called lost cause, not at all. He was never weirdly jumpy or agitated about the amount of broccoli on his plate, although he did have a weird way of describing it. He'd celebrate a victory or difficult accomplishment but was never over confident. He was never too gabby, in fact he was taciturn at times, keeping his thoughts to himself as the mood of the moment dictated. This was especially so once he cottoned onto Conrad's lies and insidious intentions. There was no doubt, though, that in all of this Forrest endured his own version of darkness.

The next perversion of truth, Alexsis pointed out, dealt with genetics. Conrad claimed Forrest inherited the disease from his father, who was manic depressive as well. Absolute bullshit Alexsis declared, asserting that her father was always even with them as kids, never extreme in his manifestations of affection for them or, for that matter, his disapproval of their misdeeds. The clincher in the gaslighting of Forrest was that he was illegitimate.

Alexsis' narrative was suddenly interrupted when a small child bobbed by, leather halter straps dragging behind him. Chasing a small wiry white pup on the loose that cut away beyond the fountain, the tyke bound about helter-skelter, scattering the pigeons feeding at the feet of the man in the straw hat. He caught the little fellow who let out a high-pitched yelp and released him to a frantic mother who had raced up in pursuit. She thanked the rescuer profusely and strode off in the direction of the arch, clutching her son in a firm embrace, halter straps dangling. Alexsis said the lad looked quite athletic in his adorable little cross-trainers while Lucy commented on his chunky calves, so like her own. The pigeons flocked back to the man in the hat and Alexsis returned to the past.

Resentful yes, but somehow Victor Troyes' children managed to cope. Isla had her books, her poetry, and her silence. Alexsis danced madly until she dropped, which she defined as her frenzied attempt to keep anger and animosity and hatred and rage against Conrad and Kat in check, and it succeeded most of the time. Forrest had his sketching and his reading, the former an extension of the latter, like with contemporary graphic novels.

Forrest read as much as Isla did. What did he read? Classic Comics. He was permitted to have them, as many as he wanted. Kat argued with Conrad that reading such trashy nonsense pacified the boy, it absorbed him, it helped take the edge off the occasional outbreak, and it distracted him from pining over the loss of his father. Virgil, the sympathetic uncle, saw to his amassing an extensive selection, from *Last of the Mohicans* and *Tom Sawyer* to *The Three Musketeers* and *Mutiny on the Bounty. The Count of Monte Cristo* and *Hamlet* appealed to Forrest the most and had the greatest influence on his thinking.

He knew all the characters in the Dumas saga and would entertain both Isla and Alexsis by telling Edmond Dantès' story over and over. The unjust imprisonment, the Abbé's instruction, the escape, the revenge. Settling of accounts intrigued Forrest.

Periodically, he claimed that he saw the ghost of his father, Victor, pleading with him to be remembered. At night, before falling asleep. Next morning he'd pull on a black t-shirt and top things off with black ball hat worn backwards and enunciate "to be or not to be" as clearly as he could. In uttering these words so precisely, he implied not his own demise, which he hadn't yet conceptualized nor contemplated, but the demise of his opponents. Nonetheless, he grasped the essential developments in Shakespeare's plot. The king and the queen were the guilty ones just like Conrad and Kat and he'd eventually see to their come-uppance. His revenge would not end in personal tragedy but in a way similar to that achieved by Edmond Dantès, the Count of Monte Cristo.

Later, when older, before they sent him away, he got even more familiar with his tragic hero by reading and rereading the actual text of Shakespeare's play that Virgil gave him. He quoted the soliloquies, in whole and in part; he had most of them memorized. It was all about berating himself for not doing anything to avenge his father's murder— what avenging his father's murder could actually be at that stage in his life he could not articulate. He'd just contort his face and gesticulate and act like he was the embodiment of stealth. He did have a firm understanding of infidelity: he followed Hamlet's lead in accusing his mother of adulterous treachery, but only within earshot of an audience comprised of two sympathetic sisters. When exiled and cut off from family, he later informed Alexsis, he cast Flex in the role of Horatio.

"So they never had Forrest sectioned?" Lucy asked after a nanny pushing a pram stopped right by their bench and inadvertently interrupted the flow of information coming from Alexsis. Three teenagers with a large sound box happened by and the pigeon man told them where to go and how to get there.

"Sectioned?" Alexsis questioned, lifting a lip to the side in puzzled uncertainty.

"Institutionalized."

"For a bit, yes." Alexsis stated, nodding, and then after a moment's silent reflection, picked up again. "Remember, Isla missed her brother just as much as I did, only she wasn't as vocal about it. Forrest as a subject of discussion in the Steele household was limited although we both were sure Kat and Conrad argued about him constantly. After all, Kat was his mother even though he'd made threats against her life, or so Kat, turning on the tears, had claimed on the date of his birthday, his fifteenth, maybe, can't be sure, a pseudo-celebration the birthday boy did not, or could not, attend.

"It was determined that Forrest suffered severely from a personality disorder and was analysed as capable of violence. I was never sure of just how that analysis was determined. Expressions of rage were not uncommon in Forrest's early teens, but I doubted the validity of defining them as violent outbursts. Conrad claimed Forrest was sick mentally and banished him, calling it a matter of family safety. So, yeah, Forrest was institutionalized for a period of time."

"Local?"

"Local, yes. Brooklyn."

"Got it."

"If it had not been for the intervention of Virgil Troyes, Candace's father," Alexsis continued, "who knows what might have happened to Forrest. He kept him out of harm's way. How, I don't know, but he did."

"I remember Virgil as being a sort of gentle giant," Lucy said, recalling time spent talking with him on the *Iphigenia*. Alexsis agreed and then unravelled more of her tale of family discord.

Kat and Virgil disagreed about Forrest and what to do with him. Her exasperation over the issue of a recalcitrant son was diminished considerably by Virgil's understanding and his more nuanced response to a delicate family problem. He'd supported Forrest over the intervening years in a lot of different ways. On the QT. It was Alexsis' considered opinion that if it were not for Virgil, and to some extent Eleni, Forrest would have likely done himself in. Alexsis confessed to learning that disturbing fact more recently.

Once sent away to boarding school, Forrest never returned to the home front. His ostracism continued well into his freshman year at college. One big deception proposed by Conrad was that Forrest was dead, having been the victim of an avalanche while skiing in Colorado, and that his body would likely not be recovered until summer, if ever. Alexsis suggested "that load of malicious crap" was concocted to make her and Isla feel more isolated and powerless and have them suffer just a little bit more their sense of having lost a brother.

"Until recently," Alexsis picked up again having allowed herself after a brief pause in the narration, "basically after what happened on the *Iphigenia*, I had no real understanding of what he went through. Not just before Bruges but after as well. We had little communication over the past decade or so. But not now, no, not now. There were periods when I did not hear from him at all. Text and emails went unanswered. Even Virgil, who kept me informed as well as he could, was limited in his ability to reach him. And Flex, with him out west, even he was unable to get through to him at times.

"I know in this day and age that our lack of communication seems improbable, but that only speaks to the power Conrad had over Isla and me. Like in the Greek plays about Orestes: the two sisters of Orestes are by and large held captive, cut off from their brother, unable to relieve the feelings of hostility caused by the murder of their father, Agamemnon, hero of the Trojan War. From what I remember from seeing the plays, Electra is the rebellious one and, ah — I forget the name of the more passive one. She's more subservient. As I suggested back there a couple of minutes ago, Electra and Orestes eventually contrive to eliminate those responsible for their collective misery, their mother and her usurping paramour. Since Bruges, I've tried to keep Forrest close, just like Electra with Orestes."

"I see the similarities."

"How do I know all this classical stuff? Remember, Lucy, I was along for those trips to Greece when we were young and saw all the same dramas Isla referred to, you know the *Oresteia*. How else? Forrest. When we get together, he unloads, it's like he unleashes on me everything he's suffering. It's absolutely frightful. In fact, it's terrifying at times."

"Why is that?"

"Forrest was, and is, haunted. Big time. Guilt, I suppose. On many accounts. He claims he is trapped in the dungeons of the damned from which there is no exit."

"Sorry?"

"Hell. And he confesses that it is the hell of his own making."

When Alexsis' phone rang, she answered it immediately and then silently mouthed the word 'office' in order that Lucy would not be left hanging. The Washington Square Arch interested Lucy, so she wandered off to take it in again while Alexsis dealt with her call. A saxophone player was entertaining a group of listeners by the arch and that was enough for Lucy. Sorry, George Washington, she muttered to herself and tuned into what she thought of as sensuous jazz. The entertainer wore a black ball cap capped with gold fleur-de-lys that caught Lucy's eye. About the time Alexsis approached, the musician moved on and what was left of the small crowd dispersed. Lucy said they were fortunate to reclaim their bench next to the pigeon man before a couple of sunbathers emerging from a spot on the grass performed an artful volte-face unable to refrain from laughing.

"As though choreographed by the memory of ghosts of the locally departed," Alexsis said.

"Not taking themselves too seriously, yeah?"

"Exactly. Okay, after Bruges it was easy to forget Conrad Steele, our false father, so pompous and seigneurial and condescending, and Kat, the mother who betrayed our real father and us, her children. As you know now well enough, Isla has her studies and her poetry and I have my haute couture designs. Forrest has his demons."

"Demons?"

"That's what I said."

And having said that, Alexsis launched again, this time into the depths of her brother's madness, its origins, its manifestations, its continuing strain on his state of mind. She attempted to explain as well as she could what plagued her benighted brother.

Chapter 17
Benighted

An aside here, divine in origin, human in direction; short but germane to establishing complete understanding of what plagued Forrest Troyes. With greater comprehension in mind, let me add to the factual information that both Isla and Alexsis presented to Lucy regarding the dire situation Orestes found himself in. Contemporary parlance has it this way: damned if he did and damned if he didn't. Having effected revenge for bloody murder it was axiomatic that he'd become a bloody murderer himself. A curse, much older than ancient syllogistic reasoning.

Though assigned the title of god of divine distance, it is, and always was, incumbent upon me as the source of all light to oversee the constitution of grand societies and the illustrious cities engendered therein and, in addition, to preside over their religious laws and rituals. A primary function of mine in this regard is and always was to make mortals aware of their guilt and having done so, purify them, if they stand accused of offense against the gods or of actions contrary to divine dictates and decrees. In addition, what should never be overlooked in all of this is the role played by Nemesis, goddess of retribution.

Thus and therefore, Orestes—

Question: How was the madness that beset Orestes made manifest? Answer: he was pursued by the Erinyes, also known in the vernacular as the Furies. Esteemed members in the circle of the immortals, the Erinyes in the context of the *Oresteia* were ancient goddesses of retribution who pursued mortals for crimes against natural law, for murder, matricide, unfilial acts of treachery, for contravening ancient laws of justice, or for gross disregard of divine precept issued forth from Olympus. They revealed themselves as hideous winged females, their eyes bloodied, their hair, arms, and waists ringed with vile and loathsome serpents that hissed and spewed out poisonous venom. Attired in long black clothing or (depending on the season, as a glib and witty poet once put it, Juvenal methinks, sinking to the lowest level of mimetic representation) in leg revealing short skirts and hunter-maiden boots (according to the fashion of the day). A victim like Orestes writhed in pain when the Erinyes mercilessly lashed his prostrate body and back, their whips so very accurate in meeting out a primitive and exacting form of payment for transgression. Born of Gaia's primal blood, these shape-shifters resided in Stygian hell, emerging when justice needed to be served, that is to say, their kind of justice. In the story of Orestes' fateful matricide, their torment of him had just begun when he wiped clean his executioner's bloody sword. The sequel to his acts of vengeance? He was forced to wander alone across ancient domains, a vagrant haunted by self-loathing, endlessly pursued by the taunting Furies.

As Alexsis might frame it, her brother to a T.

Whenever Forest Troyes thought about what he'd done, these hag-like creatures from the darkness of the netherworld confronted him in a violent flurry, shrieking, lashing out at him for his sins— parental disobedience, murder, matricide. They assumed more contemporary guises and employed 20th and 21st century innovations in the sphere of mental torture, like appearing together as omens in bad trips induced by taking LSD. He was forced to endure untold misery and misfortune, unable to escape their grip on his mind. They drove him mad. That is one way to describe what he went through. There are other ways more conducive to modern interpretation of what constituted his perturbed mental state. I leave them to research and reader imagination.

And so, Alexsis' benighted brother.

Chapter 18
Hags in Rags

Brushing a miniscule bug off the collar of her blouse with a quick flick of a finger, Alexsis declared, "I'll tell you this, Lucy, I've not spent all of my time since Bruges on the concept board at Excelsior State Designs. I researched mental health in depth, even consulted with professionals about the types of disorders that can plague individuals like Forrest. My recollections of all that Conrad declared still troubled me. I was determined to attain a clearer picture of what caused my brother's mental lapses or, analogously, his bouts of madness."

Lucy started to pose a question but trailed off, allowing Alexsis to say on.

"Bereavement and loss of a loved one," Alexsis stated authoritatively, "check." She closed her eyes then immediately opened them again. It was like a sign of emphasis, a visual exclamation point.

"Right," Lucy said. "Your father, Victor Troyes."

Alexsis picked up a leaf lying by the side of the bench, flattened it, and then began pulling it apart.

Symbolic, Lucy thought. What she was doing was enacting a metaphor for sorting things, her own mental anguish, such as it might be. Possible, but not probable.

"Childhood trauma and neglect," Alexsis continued, the leaf in her fingers like nature's abacus. "Check. Stigma and isolation. Check. Stress, compulsion, obsession, addiction. Check. Check. Check. Check."

"I get the picture, Alexsis."

"My brother Forrest Troyes to a T," she said, crunching and tossing aside what remained of the leaf.

"With all that to account for, you end up not being your own person. You have no freedom to act. Personality disorder, why not, with all that baggage? Madness, you bet."

Lucy nodded sympathetically. She noted signs of wet marking the underarms of Alexsis' blouse. She'd long been aware of the cooling effect of her own trickle-down perspiration.

"And let's not forget his absolute craving for vengeance against those who caused the ghost of his father to appear. How could he not remember him? That was just the beginning, you see, when we were all young. At times he seemed untethered from reality, which confused Isla and me. I believe

214

now it was his attempt to cross the divide that separated us kids from our rightful due."

The need to reevaluate Alexsis suddenly struck Lucy. She was revealing much about Forrest but in the process had to be unburdening herself in some subtle way of that sense of moral responsibility she held towards him. In discussing his situation in such detail like this, was she merely objectifying the psychological spin-off that resulted from criminal culpability? She was definitely no Lady Macbeth with her bloody hands suffering the soul-destroying consequences of her actions. No, not at all. Never could be. No crying out for all the perfumes of Arabia to wash away her guilt. Alexsis Troyes was the self-declared personification of insouciant disinclination— no compunction at all, thank you loads— and yet willing to reveal so much. Was it mere dramatization for effect to satisfy a reporter's enduring curiosity, like artists declaring it was art for art's sake to antagonize the critics?

Lucy wondered why she was second-guessing herself and her estimation of what Alexsis was actually achieving by letting it all spill out. What was going on? The social equivalent of a penitent kneeling before a confessor hoping to attain forgiveness for sins with only a modicum of penance to perform for the re-set; or more likely, given what Alexsis had already declared, no penance at all. Was Lucy's role again that of the empathetic confidante? Or, with the friendly surroundings of the park serving as the couch of self-revelation, that of the psychologist bound by ethical restrictions to say naught? Was it Alexsis' intention to use Lucy as a filter for truth, expecting her in the process to utter platitudes that reeked of approval? In scenes of virtual transformation, was it Alexsis' presumption that Lucy could play intermediary between judgement and sentencing once she entrusted her with restricted knowledge? On the other hand, Lucy knew that from the get-go she was wont to re-engineer all the puzzling *Iphigenia* scenes in order to arrive at a different conclusion regarding the demise of Kat.

Isla was innocent. Lucy accepted that as probable. In *Furious Truths* she had worked things out her way. Surely Alexsis would prefer to be discussing her success in the fashion industry at Excelsior State Creations with Lucy; she demurred to responding openly to queries about Bruges and its aftermath and, more importantly, the actions of her mad brother. Was making herself a different kind of open book Alexsis' way?

Lucy asked. "How did Forrest suffer from his demons?"

"Let me provide you with as complete a picture as time will allow me," Alexsis said, checking her phone and then glancing toward the arch. "I still have enough. I'll deal with Forrest's doings before but largely since Bruges. Like I said, that's when I had the most contact with him in spite of his generally antisocial stance. Not that he was ever really sociable and *that* he blames on you know who. What I saw and heard from my brother was totally distressing. I was drawn into the darkest depths of his existence, a hell I may have helped create. Inadvertently, of course, following my own mad rushes, my own need to get retribution."

At this point Alexsis listed her sources: her intense conversations with Forrest in addition to the writings and drawings he let her have; information Virgil passed on to her about his visits with him; what Flex, who was closest to Forrest, revealed about his thinking leading up to his actions against Conrad and Kat; and Candace (his beloved), who added insight where none seemed possible. Lucy was impressed. She asked about what findings counselling provided. Time permitting, they'd get to that, Alexsis replied. In drifting back she'd have to be selective.

Flex shared the following with Alexsis. Some months prior to his machinations against Conrad and Kat in real terms, Forest became obsessed with Paladin, the dark hero of *Have Gun Will Travel.* For a period of over a week, he watched old reruns of the classic western on television.

Paladin, a hitman with moral purpose operating out of a San Francisco hotel, modelled himself on the knight errant of medieval lore— heroic, courteous, purposeful. When called upon, he set out to right the wrongs inflicted upon innocent victims, intent on seeing justice done. Paladin introduced himself into the action by first presenting his calling card which featured an emblematic chess knight. Forrest was intrigued by the moral imperative that motivated this chivalrous lead character in the series and considered it more than just entertainment that reflected a bygone era in popular television viewing. He took personal meaning from every job that Paladin took on.

Flex also explained how during that same period of time Forrest induced him to watch several episodes of *Colonel Flack* that he was able to pull up through the internet. The colonel, a modern-day Robin Hood with a sidekick named Patsy, made it his business to get even with swindlers and characters of lesser ethical standing that attempted to make off with ill-gotten gains. The colonel's ability to overcome the cads, outmaneuver the charlatans, and cheat the cheaters sent Forrest snickering and clapping about the room as though he were personally involved. What he found most attractive about Colonel Flack was his propensity to manufacture Latin quotes to explain a dire situation that he and Patsy might have landed themselves in. Forrest would make up his own mumbo jumbo and then add "which means" to initiate his translation. He frequently relied on the colonel's "We have the one thing money can't buy: poverty," by which Forest meant "we lived an impoverished existence because of Conrad and Kat." Forrest complained that there were too few episodes of the old black and white show to watch and be inspired by. He berated himself for failing to take action because of moral weakness. On one occasion he blabbered something obscure and virtually incomprehensible that he insisted was Greek and then translated: "Indolence, thy name is Forrest." On another occasion he repeated the phrase *agenbite of inwit* many times over but was unable to explain its meaning.

The typological unspooling of material to explain Forrest Troyes continued with Alexsis' revelations, what she termed first-hand encounters. She remembered an incident from their younger days. Forrest told her that when in middle school and into sports he'd see Conrad in the face of his opposition. Reactions: fear and trepidation on the one hand, and on the other hand physical attack with the intention of inflicting serious harm on the first kid he had to tackle. An anecdote she called it, "exposing the impulses of his awakened reptile brain." He'd see Conrad's despicable face in soapy bubbles, in puddles enroute to school, in mirrors and even in mirror fragments that bloodied his fingertips.

There was the BMW experience from back before the exile. Conrad told Forrest to exchange places with Boyd Alexander because he was old enough to know how the gear shift worked. Forrest refused to sit in the driver's seat, not because he wouldn't like to, but because it was a putdown in the making. He knew it was an attempt on Conrad's part to belittle him in front of Boyd Alexander who, though younger, was taller and could reach the pedals with ease. Forest dreamed later of driving the car over Conrad's prostrate body but, sadly, as an angered driver riding roughshod through the nightscape of reprisal, he encountered nothing but roadblocks and foggy cul-de-sacs.

During the decade of his forced disengagement from family, the seeds of vengeance, planted early in his life, germinated and grew large enough to completely overwhelm his thoughts, his daylight reveries, his very being in the world. Fever dreams filled with obscenities dominated his nights, all part of a psychodrama in which he played both victim and tyrant, abuser and abused. He felt judged guilty and condemned to make what was broken whole again— or else!— but he knew not how to do so. Set adrift in the immensity of despair, he turned to drugs, reached low threshold highs and took psychotropic trips where he came face to face with the gaping void. He experimented with meth, cocaine, heroin: substance abuse became a byword for motivational research. Flex explained that during that lamentable period it was as though a multi-headed and violent creature, in possession of Forrest's mind and will, had led his dear friend to the very edge of self-destruction. On more than one occasion Forrest threatened suicide for failing to fulfill his destiny.

Desolation circumscribed his every day: confusion, disorientation, destructive behaviour. Forrest recorded in detail how he felt trapped in quicksand and every effort to move was stymied. He was a mouse caught in a maze. He was forever ascending and descending an Escher staircase. Any movement towards reclaiming normalcy or reality of the most basic order spiraled into justification for his need of revenge. Seeing Conrad Steele lying on a slab would secure his escape. It would be his vindication. It would validate all he had had to suffer.

As was the case when younger, Forrest found temporary release in reading. The world he sought therein had now expanded considerably. He sought to explore established interests, but with themes developed outside of established genres. The hardnosed protagonists of Raymond Chandler added viability to what had been overly long in coming to a conclusion in the world that Hamlet inhabited. He understood Hamlet's dilemma, of course— certainty of action and the perfect opportunity to strike— and he understood his love-hate relationship with his disloyal mother. The play's the thing. But what was *his* play? Whatever it proved to be beyond introverted self-abasement, it would have to eschew protracted intellectual analysis. Or what passed for it.

He delved into Dostoevsky's *Crime and Punishment* and identified immediately with Raskolnikov, the protagonist who believed he had special status and could take on the spiritual weight of employing evil means to achieve humanitarian ends. What was appealing about Raskolnikov, despite the feverous days of delirium he subsequently endured, was that he had already engaged in violent action. Unlike him, Forrest maintained, he had nothing bloody to confess and therefore was not yet worthy of redemption, the possible exception being his mortal sin of omission, namely, not avenging his father's murder. Other readings along similar lines forced him to consider the long-standing ethical question: Could one do the wrong thing for the right reason, or the right thing for the wrong reason? Yes, Forrest reasoned, like Raskolnikov, one could. He attempted in more lucid moments, rare though they were, to establish a rationale for such action that went beyond revenge. His attempts to do so failed.

Isolation and alienation delivered intermittent consolation. When terror eased its grip on Forrest, a conceited belief of possessing superior intelligence asserted itself. And then as though encouraged by divine infusion, he reverted back to boyhood fascination and took up again the story of Orestes' revenge. It obsessed him, it comforted him, it filled him with hope. Days, months, years of woeful disconsolation faded into a Mycenaean mist.

News of the Amsterdam to Bruges cycling excursion the family was undertaking elated him. He embraced the idea of finally being proactive and of fulfilling his destiny. Fate had tapped him on the shoulder. All he required was an effective plan of action. He had dependable connections. Flex was onboard and assured him that Alexsis would be as well. He'd quit the west coast and arrive covertly in Europe as Richard Boone. After Bruges, he'd escape to New York and begin life anew. Forrest Troyes exulted in the belief that remission from years of demeaning ostracization was a now real possibility.

The relapse began with serial nightmares where Dolf Van Handelaar's elongated Urban Dart plunged into the canal at the stern of the *Iphigenia*. It contained not Conrad Steele but Forrest himself, writhing creatures spitting venomous accusations at him. In some versions of the disturbing dream, the imagery morphed into a scene where Forrest was set adrift in a pool of piranhas, the band of blue overhead that he, as dreamer, reached for could never be reached. The exaltation he had experienced withered away in a couple of New York seconds. That familiar, malignant force, believed expunged by a bloody hand on a foreign shore, had recaptured his mind ipso facto and filled it again with the ineluctable modalities of conscience, the most potent of which remained guilt. Agenbite of inwit.

Guilt assumed innumerable interior voices: primarily that of Kat, Conrad shadowing her and echoing her cries and curses; that of a chorus of the inexplicably offended included siblings and Candace, all accusing him of not keeping faith; Flex charging him with exploiting their friendship and Virgil with gross ingratitude. Even Dolf Van Handelaar, hooded and waving a crooked finger, called him out constantly for betraying him and sending him to prison. When reason prevailed, Forrest could account only for the charge of matricide. He admitted that he had been trapped by circumstances beyond his conscious control, that he'd lived his life under duress, and that he was morally obliged to seek justifiable revenge. Guilt produced a host of additional day-light hallucinations, most immersed in fear and paranoia.

Peaceful sleep escaped him completely. The well-appointed living quarters that Alexsis had arranged for him close to hers he called a shithole. Virgil reported him as having lain virtually naked on a couch for extended periods of time, passing as much as six days without food or drink, his shaved head buried in a red toque. Alexsis caught him trying to bite off a finger. She claimed he recovered well enough from other attempts at self-mutilation. Flex reported Forrest needing to have his "head on a swivel" trying to keep track of the monster with a thousand faces that had taken up residence in his apartment. Isla described his self-inflicted isolation as that of an anchorite submissive to an obscure ideal, an atmosphere of fear surrounding its apprehension. The walls of his living room supposedly closed in on him. Darkness flooded into the washroom even with all the lights on.

Sleep disorders were considered by all concerned as being central to Forrest's destructive state of mind, from insomnia to bruxism, to restless leg syndrome. Ironically, narcolepsy held but a futile hope. Subsequently, light therapy was suggested as a possible fix for the sleep-wake disorder he was thought to be suffering from: his circadian rhythm never recovered from the European time zone differential. Theory was discarded as too far out. SAD or seasonal affective disorder got some play in the minds of the would-be rescuers. The light box that Virgil produced did no more, unfortunately, than give Forrest wilder and more frequent headaches. The idea as remedial was abandoned. Busted by the blinding light Isla argued. No sleep for the wicked was Forrest's counterargument.

Nightmares and hallucinations, released from the darkest chambers of Forrest's brain, continued. He wandered figuratively in a labyrinth of imagined threat; he wandered literally through the precincts of Central Park when he let himself out. Wherever he roamed, he encountered "hags in rags" poking him with accusations, assailing him for being a criminal on the loose. In the elevator, chanting spooks caused him to lose balance and trip over the threshold of undignified disgrace. Candace encouraged him to find a confessor and thereby be released from the spiritual hell he inhabited— a possibility, but not a likely one.

"I'll add this," Alexsis said, glancing briefly at her watch. "Forrest subjected himself to months of psychoanalysis at various mental health clinics. I encouraged him to do so. Conclusions were no more than labels: homicidal derangement, psychopathic revenge, Oedipus complex, etc. Nothing new there. He even underwent hypnosis. To no avail, just comic scenarios and ridiculous antics."

"So nothing worthwhile out of all this time spent with professionals?"

"He was encouraged to keep a written record of his thoughts and sensations and the like, you know, the ups and downs of his life since Bruges as I have outlined to you here, even suicidal impulses. Nothing new there either. He'd filled journals doing much the same since he was a kid. I keep them for him in case he takes it into his muddled head to destroy them."

"Right, you've mentioned how he pulled his drawings and doodles into his iterations."

"Look, you're at the Beverley. I'll send a sample of his recent sketches over to your hotel by courier. I use the service all the time. As long as I get the sketchbook back."

"Righto."

"That way you might get even greater insight into just who my beloved Forest Troyes is. Perceptions of terror are what you will find between the covers. Splashes of crushed slush and slime sans fruit colouring causing a flush of goosebumps is how Isla described some of his stuff. Something like that anyway. It's like, you know, a caricature of human anguish and malaise of the mind. Despite her generally mild manner, Isla is quite capable of sardonic observations. You know, the poet in her.

"Insightful she is, then."

"Very. Walk with me now through the arch towards Fifth Avenue. I'll hail a taxi there and get back to the office."

"No further skiving off, yeah?"

"Exactly. And no rest for the wicked either."

"I've heard that one before."

"You see, Lucy," Alexsis said, rising from the bench, "Forrest believes, as I do, that what transpired in Bruges was ordained, by a higher power, if you will, and therefore morally justified. He was never maliciously vindictive, just motivated by something he had no control over. Let's call it his fate. His virtual mental breakdown still mystifies all of us concerned with his welfare."

"Right. Right."

"There's so much more I could tell you, but I must get going now. I haven't said too much about what I went through. Material for another day, I suppose."

"I understand completely."

"It's like in the Orestes story that Isla alluded to. Orestes chose the action Apollo sanctioned. Also, his sister Electra aided and abetted him. Together they were complicit in the execution of their father's murderers. Clytemnestra, their faithless mother, also fell victim to their vengeance."

"And by extension, that implicates you, Alexsis, yeah?"

"Correct."

After some thought Lucy asked, "Am I to understand, then, that you and your brother Forrest are guilty of both homicide and matricide?"

"Correct."

"And that's the absolute truth then."

"The bottom line. That's what you wanted all along, isn't it, the bottom line?"

"That's another way of phrasing it. But accurate enough, yeah."

Alexsis gave Lucy shrewd look of estimation then added, "Don't omit the part Flex played. He'd be disappointed if you left him out of your calculations."

"Right. We're referring to the chap as Flex, but that's just a nickname if I recall correctly.

"He's Fletcher Christian. Forrest's buddy for years. We've always called him Flex."

"I can recall Conrad referring to him as 'that upstart parvenu.' Yeah, that's what he called him."

"Flex agonized for nearly two decades over Forrest's dire situation. Believe me, he would willingly battle against any excoriation of his longtime friend."

"Right. Old Mack the Knife himself. The cloud hanging over your head lifted when he arrived on the *Iphigenia*, yeah?"

Lucy remembered how Alexsis had thrown off her dark attire for an aqua blue, long flowing shift. She called it a chiton.

"Absolutely. Don't forget your promise."

"Promise?"

"To keep your word," Alexsis answered and then smiling added, "to protect your sources, you know like what a reporter does when hassled by the police to explain things reported."

Under the afternoon sun, Alexsis' olive complexion appeared highlighted in silver. She looked relieved.

"Righto, keep schtum."

Arranging how to get and return Forrest's sketchbook, Lucy Hunter and Alexsis Troyes said their goodbyes.

Chapter 19
Chiaroscuro Grotesques

As soon as Alexsis disappeared in a yellow blur around the corner of Fifth Avenue, Lucy decided that she wasn't going to skive off either. She headed along Beverley Place to the 4TO bookstore at a determined pace and got there breathless with expectation. She wanted to procure a copy of the *Oresteia*. One was found on a top shelf of the Classics section. A hands-on reading of Aeschylus' trilogy. Brilliant! Any gaps in her appreciation of the three tragedies that might arise she could fill in by accessing internet criticism. Arriving at the hotel, she was notified that a small package had been delivered for her. Lucy Hunter, investigative reporter par excellence, anticipated a protracted night of reading and research.

Entering her room, she greeted herself in the mirror and, contemplating the reflection shining there, wondered if she had changed in any way since morning, knowing what she now knew about what so intrigued her regarding the Troyes tragedies since arriving in NYC— the bottom line, as Alexsis had phrased it. What she saw was the universal shrug of the undecided. But then that familiar reflection with a shake of her head posed questions about moral responsibility. Was she, reporter ever in pursuit of truth, to condone by her silence the crimes Alexsis confessed? She and Forrest and Flex were responsible for a double homicide. Was she actually to remain schtum in the face of incontrovertible fact? Indeed, what had been Alexsis' motivation in telling all? And Lucy's reflection answered with the shrug of the morally conflicted.

Dumping her daypack where convenient, she formulated a likely concatenation for the evening's activities. After a quick perusal of Forrest's book, she would read the first two tragedies of the *Oresteia,* order in food and drink from the Four Square Restaurant with chocolate pudding for dessert, delve into the sketches after that, and then round out the night reading the third play.

Isla and Alexsis had outlined extremely well what Forest had to endure in his life both before and after Bruges. With that as a given, Lucy regarded the sketchbook now in her possession as an alternate way of accessing the workings of his mind. The first look in left her with the impression that his artwork so-called was noir in the extreme. She'd get back to it after her pudding, should she be fortunate enough to have any delivered with the rest of her order. She picked up the *Oresteia,* read the general introduction, then got into the first play, which dramatized the bloody murder of Agamemnon and Cassandra at the hands of his wife Clytemnestra and her lover. In just over an hour, she'd finished *Agamemnon* and began *The Libation Bearers,* which dramatized the execution of Clytemnestra and her conniving consort Aegisthus at the hands of Orestes and Electra. *Agamemnon* and *The Libation Bearers* confirmed first-hand her minimal knowledge about the curse of the House of Atreus. She took no notes. Just as Isla and Alexsis asserted: Orestes found himself trapped in a moral bind that plagued him beyond reason. He was caught in the paradoxical web of antinomies. His final choice of action, which did involve slaying his mother, led to guilt about violating sacred principles. Pursued by the Furies, madness enveloped him completely.

Forest's sketchbook. Perceptions of terror in stark black and white was how Alexsis had described the contents and, having taken time to dissect each page as objectively as she could, Lucy decided Alexsis was absolutely right. What she had in her hands was a portfolio of chiaroscuro grotesques: madness made manifest in a manic clash of dark and light. The sketchbook presented her with a sequence of gestalt-like splashes of psychopathic derangement, what could only be the product of delirium and hysteria. Vipers and assorted forms of fanged phantasmagoria, murky shapes, severed fingers, hideous ink and wash self-portraits, all emerging out of Forrest's haunted imagination, the uber surreal representations of a fractured mind. Peripheral texts scattered helter-skelter in a scribbled hand offered obscure esoteric commentary. *Agenbite of inwit* was decipherable on a couple of pages. The texts, Lucy reasoned, pointed to the possibility that Forrest, having confronted and captured in charcoal lines and random smudges the subject of his nightmare or hallucination, was attempting to analyze it in familiar language so as to control it, but the drawings had a language all their own. She made out one significant scrawled notation on a page opposite a montage of Gorgon-like creatures dripping black ooze and blood, the enigmatic "no vocabulary for names that cannot be spoken." After fifteen minutes or so of close scrutiny, Lucy had had enough.

She recalled experiencing the same kind of visceral reaction when scanning Victor Hugo's graphic prints as requested to do so by photographer associate Vanessa De La Croix who was assigned to research images of bedlam for a medical journal. Trawling through the mephitic miasma of a decomposing mind had not been easy then. It was not easy now.

Lucy thought twice about ordering food in but the idea of another pastrami on rye overcame any resistance that exploring Forrest's dark and dreary mindscape may have given rise to, gut reaction notwithstanding.

"Pile on the pickles, yeah?" she shouted into the phone. "Bottled water. And a pudding, chocolate preferably. If not available, bread pudding will do. But with lots of raisins."

Responding to the voice at the other end of the line, she said, "Righto, trifle will do. With custard, yeah?"

When she finished reading the introduction to the last play of the Oresteia, Lucy decided she was too tired to get into it, that she'd read it at the airport or on the flight back to London. Her thoughts drifted back to the sketchbook.

Concrete evidence of a mad attempt at purging, was that what Forrest's demented drawings and inscrutable scribbles amounted to? Lucy pondered just such a possibility in an attempt to make sense of a pattern repeated. A perverse kind of objective correlative for *mea culpa* and remorseful self-reproach? Was she being impetuous in thinking so? Was she engaging once again in apophenia? Orestes and Forrest Troyes: the two narratives mirrored each other in terms of cause and effect. Murder then madness. She had much to consider before calling it a night, but at this point she was content to answer the knock on the door and accept her order from Four

Square. She tipped the shag-haired delivery
boy surprisingly well, a kind of reflex action
at seeing a normal person doing a normal
thing.

Chapter 20
Moot Considerations

Forrest Troyes vis á vis Orestes of the House of Atreus? True, they are alike with respect to the parallels that Lucy Hunter could not help herself from drawing between them. No cynosure, I! However, well noted by now is my propensity to inspire champions of truth in the arts and sciences and (to some degree) in politics. In my capacity as immortal director of civil order and the administration of justice, I motivated both Orestes and Forrest to take similar kinds of action in reprisal for their fathers' murders.

How did I influence Forrest? I inspired him to read. I encouraged his curiosity. He was free to choose, of course, what most appealed to him given the circumstance of his life. If the declarations of twenty-first century life sciences are to be believed, the notion of free will has been debunked. Where does that leave Forrest Troyes? Something to be considered but all in good time. Be that as it may, I might have directed him to understand the wisdom in the Marcus Aurelius declaration that "The best revenge is to be unlike him who performed the injury." Sadly, I did not. Or have him consider the profound truth in Sophocles warning mortals that "All concerns of men go wrong when they wish to cure evil with evil." But alas. Be it understood that what the Fates have ordained always comes to pass. I fear contradicting or violating their dictates, always have, always will. Consider the fateful fall of Oedipus.

Plagued all his young life by the raging realization that his father was brutally eliminated at the behest of Kat and Conrad Steele, Forest was psychologically terrorized into planning and effecting murderous acts of reprisal. Fact. "The devil made him do it," to borrow an aphorism used widely in contemporary courtroom defences. Forrest was not autonomous in his actions but dominated by a force superior in strength to his ability to resist. I claim responsibility here. Based on my long-standing knowledge of established norms of justice and retribution, I approved his right to act, his mental incapacity notwithstanding. Innocent, until proven guilty beyond a reasonable doubt.

The point is this: both Orestes and Forrest were fated to go mad. Orestes was hounded by the Furies. Fact. As to Forrest, mad, yes, due to gross feelings of guilt—*agenbite of inwit* again. However, the question of culpability still remains.

Allow me at this juncture to draw a distinction between Orestes and Forrest with respect to the concept of the Aristotelian tragic hero. Any one of the many literary critics that I have inspired could reasonably argue that Orestes fits the bill. Orestes' fatal flaw, as such, is not so much a moral deficiency or excessive pride. His problems arise when he is required to make a difficult choice, one that Fate imposed upon him in the form of a long-standing family curse. Like with Oedipus, Orestes' fate is sealed. Does he suffer more than he deserves? Debatable. As to Forrest Troyes, it would be more challenging to legitimately cast him in the role of tragic hero even though he suffers greatly. Obsession as fatal flaw? Possibly. Family curse? None evident. Epigenetic inheritance? That would be a long shot. And where on his part is the recognition, what Aristotle calls anagnorisis? Moot considerations, indeed. On this point, I might have had Forrest Troyes discover the ancient and oft repeated proverb that "Whom the gods would destroy they first make mad." Beyond the parameters of Aristotelian theory, Orestes experiences redemption. Will Forrest?

But I digress. After all, this is not so much a story of my magnanimity as it is one of Lucy Hunter's fate to judge fairly and unequivocally Forrest Troyes for his treacherous matricide. For the record, and as she herself hinted at, the world that

Alexsis inhabited prior to events on the *Iphigenia* provides matter for another day or, to put it more succinctly, matter for another play. Consult Sophocles. Contemporary theory maintains that felt emotion can be defined as a biochemical algorithm actively engaging cerebral matter. I maintain that madness has myriad manifestations.

Chapter 21
Schtum

Morning ablutions seen to, Lucy conned herself into preparing a cup of packaged house tea with the understanding that it would probably help her get a start on the day in the right frame of mind. Traipsing around in the cotton waffle bathrobe, she looked for and found her tablet. It had fallen between the bed and the nightstand. Her phone was easier to find. Tea as bracer, she sat down at the rolltop desk and checked for emails. One contained a greeting from Vanessa De La Croix in Paris. "Report on autocracy on the mark" read a message from the Bureau. Another informed her that her scheduled flight back to London would be delayed a couple of hours, from six PM to eight PM. The delay would factor into how she spent her last day in the village.

The tea proved satisfying enough when initial slurping eased to slow sipping. Lucy drifted into remembering fragments of a dream that she determined was a reflection of the previous night's activity, in particular her close reading of *The Libation Bearers*.

Her oneiric persona was participating in a choral funeral procession that transformed itself into a frenzied scene of rage and grief and piercing cries for revenge. Impending death was foreshadowed when a strand of hair mutated into a vile and vicious serpent. Cups of blood were poured over a grave while a hooded figure read from a book of curses. Angry crones appeared out of the swirling vortex decrying matricide.

Puzzling over the interpretation of the dream images, Lucy decided to research the Orestes Complex. The several sites she consulted on the internet provided her with little more than a species of clinical definition and a token amount of Freudian jargon. She concluded that Forrest Troyes' sketchbook was probably more insightful. She'd leave the sketchbook with the desk clerk as had been arranged with Alexsis the previous day. In the back of Lucy's mind: what to do with the information she now had about the demise of Conrad and Kat Steele and those morally and legally responsible for bringing it about. Truth be known, she was of two minds. Decisions, decisions.

An easier decision concerned the immediate: she was capable of calculating the use of the remaining hours in her New York City sojourn right down to the last minute and that included how long it would take to get out to Kennedy International. Calling on Alexsis? No, there was not much more she could reveal about Forrest. Then again, perhaps more about herself? Haute couture, not significant in Lucy's range of interests. A nonstarter. As previously thought, she would begin the *Eumenides* at the airport and finish it on the flight home. Meanwhile she would put her sensible walking shoes to good use and allow her interior flâneuse to get a little more exterior stimulation and just maybe in the process she'd come to some resolution about making the moral judgement she knew she'd have to make. Destinations: the Whitney Museum and a last Yemeni latte at the Bistro Massimo. Her packed valise, readied for departure, she'd leave at the Beverley reception desk.

She got to Greenwich Avenue then headed west to Jackson Square where she sat to appreciate the fountain, resting all the while. She took in the sights along Horatio then turned up Washington Street, making her way to the Whitney Museum of American Art. She felt content knowing she'd worn suitable attire for the visit though perhaps her pseudo business combo of blazer, blouse, and tailored slacks would prove unnecessarily formal for the long London flight late in the day. She snickered at the incongruity of the daypack hung over her shoulder, that well-travelled accoutrement worthy at present of haute couture recognition. Leaving it at the coat check as requested, she proceeded immediately to the seventh floor of the museum where many works by Edward Hooper hung and from which she had to drag herself away, given that she had but two hours to enjoy all of the exhibition. Time took flight, carrying an elated and observant Lucy with it. She could not help periodically attempting to project Edward Hopper's depictions of isolation, which she found intriguing in themselves, onto the canvas of Forrest Troyes' reality. Not an easy association but a compelling one.

The track back towards Bistro Massimo led her along Gansevoort where she turned right and sauntered along Hudson as far as Abington Square Park which she considered an oasis of green in the midst of a busy neighbourhood, Edward Hooper territory. For such an urban complexity of wrought iron and concrete and pavement, Lucy was pleased to observe, there was plenty of lush green. Shade trees were ubiquitous. She might have rested in Abington Square Park or taken coffee at any number of cafés she passed along the way, but she was determined to keep to her schedule in reaching the bistro where she hoped to engage Bert one last time. Her only delay along Bleecker Street occurred when she stopped to peruse titles in the Bookmarc outdoor bins, corner of West Eleventh.

Bleecker Street with its elaborate green cycling lane induced random recollections of cycling with Alexsis and others along the bike routes in the Lowlands.

And, naturally enough, murder raised its ambiguous head, leaving Lucy still unresolved about how to deal with information she promised to keep to herself. She'd had more than one jolt of scruples since starting out from the Beverley. These she considered head rushes of cerebral incitement fusing judgement and moral certitude. Before she consulted her watch again, Lucy was sitting at a table in the familiar outdoor terrasse watching Bert serve a table of four.

Her daypack hooked over the back of a chair, Lucy breathed in deeply—emanations so redolent of the Med she remembered, jasmine here, the fragrant scent of the hyacinth there, the aroma of cooked garlic bringing all down to earth. When Bert delivered the Yemeni latte, she said, "Full circle, ending where it began."

"Yes, ma'am. Lucy. Attractive young women with you yesterday."

"You got their attention well enough, Bert. Now that bloke with the craggy face and rifled hair, tattoos, chewing an unlit matchstick."

"Best left unlit."

"Right, best before, as it were, mate. He came in yesterday just as we were leaving. Who? What? Why?"

"Emerson Holmes. He was my prof for a course in political philosophy. Best ever. Yesterday, I had him sign my copy of *Variations in the Socratic Dialogue*, which

245

he wrote, apparently, when he was not much older than I am now."

"I must confess to misjudging the chap. I jumped to the most improbable conclusions about him."

"Many do."

"Looks can be deceiving, yeah?"

Lucy fell to berating herself, knowing that more than once she'd been taken to task for being too quick to judge. She shook her head slightly, snickering at the thought of just how ridiculously off the mark her initial estimation of the bloke had been.

"Porn star," she said in response to Bert's quizzical look.

"I see why you're sniggering. Centuries ago, Plato advocated getting beyond biases and flawed assumptions."

"In dealing with humans, it's the same old, same old, like in falling back on a cliché to express an idea or a regret."

"'Riddle me this,' Professor Holmes said to our class one particular session: 'Does empirical proof engender empirical profundities?'"

"Does it?"

"I've been wrestling with the question ever since."

"As I would be. 'Riddle me this...' is like what a supplicant at Apollo's shrine might have to say to get mantic mumbo-jumbo interpreted correctly."

"Professor Holmes is a bit like Apollo. A source of intellectual light. He is a very well-respected authority on classical Greek philosophy. Has a number of erudite books to his credit. *An Introduction to the pre-Socratics* is critically acclaimed. Apparently, his *Variations in the Socratic Dialogue* (that I had him sign) is a must for anyone contemplating teaching as a career. From what I understand, his best known work is *A Treatise on Plato's Republic*."

"Empirical proof of your prof's profundities, yeah?"

"True enough. Ever happen in your role as an investigative reporter that you got it wrong? As in judging if a story fits? Do you ever have to wrestle with yourself (or your publisher) over a question of social responsibility?"

"To say nothing of moral responsibility. As my good friend and associate often puts it: we work to undermine the structures in place that reward the wicked and exploit the weak. Exercising judgement is always in play. From time to time, I've been accused of overindulging in speculation, seeing a presumed relationship between things that might not be related at all."

"Doing that would necessarily bring consequences, and not always favourable ones. Right?"

"Quite. That's where discretion comes in, especially on the part of the publisher. Situations arise where I, as the reporter in search of truth, or empirical fact, if you will, feel morally obligated to publish material that might compromise my personal safety."

"And that's happened, has it?"

"I wrote an article about the Russian influence on Brexit that brought me all kinds of grief from the Brexit people. I thought I was being objective, balancing points on both sides of the question, although I personally favoured remaining with the EU."

"The other side prevailed, right?"

"Right you are. Not only that, it's impossible to describe the extent of corruption in British high society vis à vis Russian oligarchs and their filthy lucre. When the Russkies are involved, discretion really is the better part of valour. They retaliate with lethal poison even if one of their many money laundering schemes gets exposed. I ventured into that territory all civic minded and ethically charged. Regrets, nothing but regrets."

"What happened?"

"Let's just say I got more than blacklisted after I wrote up the first in what I intended to be a series of articles on that subject."

"More than blacklisted? Like threats?"

"Threats, yes. Consider the assassinations of whistle blowers by the Russian mafia, hit squads, or secret police — deaths egregiously termed suicides by British authorities. Only the strong remain unfazed by threats of retaliation. I had to get sorted. At one point I was challenged by an officious little blighter that maybe I came down too strongly on the side of righteousness against moral flexibility."

"Sounds like a reasonable observation given what some nefarious publications put out. And the internet is rife with seemingly palatable bullshit."

"Same at home. Egregious knavery, conservatives mostly, the iterations of polemicists and apologists on the right."

"How do you know where to go and what to search for?"

"Random luck provided from on high, but I avoid sentimental tosh and fashionable buzzwords. Bureau directions, to be precise. My report on Autocracy is carbon neutral, so to say. It won't instigate any death threats and so no heart pounding madly, no ears throbbing, no blood rushing crazily though the system."

"So no hard-driving imperative to tell it like it is."

"Not when it comes to the signs of an incipient oligarchy we're witnessing on a daily basis. On the other hand, I find myself in a kind of moral bind right now. Very troubling, I daresay."

"What's the issue?"

"I really can't go into the details. It involves the family of the two women you served here yesterday. I promised to keep schtum."

"Schtum?"

"Keep mum. Keep my mouth shut. In this case, keeping my mouth shut is *my* choice. Judgement again. A kind of biased curiosity got the better of me trying to prove a theory about some sinister event and now I'm paying for it with a smattering of self-torture."

"Remember what Plato said about the unexamined life and reaching beyond predilection and erroneous supposition."

"I'm examining both sides of the question. The best I've come up with so far is damned if I do and damned if I don't."

"A common enough emotional dilemma when making a crucial decision that pulls you two ways."

"Righto, Bert."

"Professor Holmes also came out with this gem. 'No one I've met rides an elevator to listen to the music.' What do you think, Lucy?"

"I'll give it some serious thought. I've an hour or two before heading to the airport. We can dissect the possibilities, yeah?"

Bert was laughing as he entered the bistro, a loaded tray in his hands.

Another exchange between Lucy and Bert entailed finding the connection between autocracy and oligarchy. This naturally led to concerns about the forthcoming election. Bert was distraught at the possibility that for a loose majority of voters the election would only be about the cost of gas, a pound of bacon and a dozen eggs. Factor into the results of the vote affluent ignorance.

"Does the bistro have any uncluttered square footage?" Lucy asked, initiating a brief bit of q and a with Bert.

"None that I know of. Why?"

"I need to lead the hobbyhorse of my moral sensibilities into the pasture of some basement storage space. I tire frequently of riding too hard."

"I'll look inside for you."

A further give and take for Lucy and Bert began with her saying, "I've often wondered about what a bistro is as opposed to a trattoria. Well, not that often, but today yes, as I approached. Can you explain the difference between the two."

"As far as I know, Lucy, a bistro is a small, relatively simple restaurant offering modest but delicious cuisine. French often. Also locally inspired dishes. Cozy. Casual. Pleasing ambiance. Such is this establishment."

"And a trattoria?"

"Is more of an Italian restaurant serving a variety of simple dishes. Informal setting, but also comfortable, accommodating, and cozy. Such is this establishment. The point is, Lucy, you leave both kinds of restaurants less hungry than when you came in."

"That's brilliant, Bert," Lucy said agreeably. "That depends on your choice of fare, mind."

"Fair comment, Lucy."

"Bring me the menu, yeah?"

And thus Lucy Hunter's last visit to the Bistro Massimo proceeded. When she finally took her leave, she said to Bert standing with arms akimbo by the door, "Young man, I leave the pursuit of eternal verities in your good hands."

Chapter 22
Airbus A350

JFK International, Terminal 8: Lucy Hunter's priority pass gave her access to all the amenities in the Greenwich Lounge. Food. Drink. View. Though impressed yet again by her up-scale surroundings, she tended to be selective when able to indulge in lavish offerings. She never considered herself too much more than ordinary, plebeian rather than patrician. Sufficient time remained before the flight was scheduled to depart, so why not play the patrician if only for the duration of a brew or two. She ordered herself a pint of Guinness and found a comfortable seat with attached side table situated in front of a large picture window that provided a view to arriving and departing aircraft.

Enjoying her Guinness, Lucy focused on her reading. She was only minimally distracted by a bevy of well-attired patricians who took possession of a section of the bar where they held forth on the coming US election, some apparently liberal in their political views and others less liberated.

Loud guffaws from the near end of the bar gave Lucy a start. A middle-aged couple were watching something like court proceedings on television. The judge overseeing the drama was a stern-faced woman, totally engaged in banging her gavel.

Lucy re-read the introduction to the *Eumenides* to refresh her understanding of Aeschylus' purpose: the play illustrated the nature of justice, the upshot being that a new order tempered by mercy and understanding was established by the court of Athens. It was based on rationality and impartiality as opposed to the Lex Talionis of blood for blood. Apollo's shrine in Delphi and the court of Areopagus in Athens divide the dramatic action of the third play in the trilogy.

As the action of the *Eumenides* begins, Apollo stands by Orestes, whom the raging Furies continue to attack; he acknowledges his influence as oracle in having Orestes commit matricide according to the will of Father Zeus. The ensuing argument, centering on Orestes' bloody action and its consequences, pits old against new, the matriarchal vs the patriarchal approach to justice.

With the announcement for boarding her particular flight, Lucy checked her phone for messages, set it to airplane mode and then made her way to where in the terminal she needed to go. She knew how detailed boarding a big jet could be. She also knew how to maneuver in order to get seated quickly.

Lucy reserved a window seat whenever she could no matter the duration of the flight. On this one, the seat next to hers remained empty. The young man occupying the aisle seat offered Lucy a smile when he arrived, which she gladly reciprocated. A few pleasantries were exchanged. Then sitting down, he plugged into some media offering the aircraft provided, a movie Lucy's thought. To her way of thinking, he could have passed for Bert's brother.

Not long after the Airbus A350 was airborne, drinks were served and shortly after that a light meal. Lucy had what the attendant assured her was proper English tea. Somewhere over the western Atlantic, she pulled her book out of her daypack that she stashed under the seat ahead and picked up reading the *Eumenides* from where she left off.

When the scene shifts from Delphi to the domain of Athena, the goddess of wisdom, Apollo carries on defending Orestes' position, claiming that he has been purified through suffering and isolation. In the collective voice of the Chorus, the Furies object, insisting most vehemently that their rights as ancient overseers of traditional justice will be violated if Orestes is cleared of culpability. Athena bids Orestes tell his story; the Furies challenge him as having behaved contrary to the laws of nature. Athena then establishes an unbiased jury of mortals to evaluate the case. The result: six for and six against. Athena casts the deciding vote in favour of Orestes. The Furies rage. Athena secures their cooperation through flattery and the promise of honours to come: henceforth they will to be called the *Eumenides*, the kindly ones. Orestes is free to follow his destiny.

"Hmm," Lucy said, closing her copy of the *Oresteia*, but nobody heard her. It was as though she needed to read the third play again in order to get it right. "Riddle me this..." She looked out the portal into the evening twilight, then pulled the shade down. She had hours to go before getting back to London and, as was her wont on long fights, drifted off as the drone of the big jet engines lulled her to sleep.

Chapter 23
Doppelgänger Bert

I might have inspired the highflying Lucy Hunter before she fell asleep to plug into some soothing music in order to effect a meditative state of mind, my favourite ethereal strains, for instance; in other words, I might have prompted her to transform the hard edges of intellectual scrutiny into sensations of well-meaning and empathic connection. Even elevator music, the butt of a recent joke, might have raised her soul to a level where she would enjoy the benefits of the god frequency. Alas, I did not move her in any of these ways. Metaphorically speaking, I had something else up my sleeve.

In working out the plan, I called upon Morpheus, the god of dreams, son of Hypnos, the god of sleep. Informed of what I had in mind and how my designs for Lucy Hunter should unfold, he immediately jumped onboard the rapid express out of the underworld of Erebus and came to my assistance, delighted to be playing a part so perfectly suited to his talents. Dreams are the means whereby humans become aware of our influences in their lives, a long-regarded belief, be it noted again, with respect to the divine infusion of light and all associated with it. Morpheus is a shapeshifter, capable of having the dreamer, in this instance, Lucy Hunter, believe the human form he assumes is real, in this instance, the Bert lookalike sitting one seat over. An ideal cut-out for my sympathetic self.

Recall how I was instrumental in the way Lucy, absolutely knackered, to use her expression, drifted off into euphoric restfulness while listening to Chopin's Nocturnes. Her contemplation of divine input, that is to say, her vision of my performance under the laurel tree, was flattering, to say the least. Also recall that I am the Nietzschean master of illusion.

Echoing Plato's Socrates, the Roman poet Juvenal in his Satires posed a familiar question that translates loosely as follows: "Who will guard the guards?" Lucy Hunter, who in her life's work has tried to answer that question, will raise the stakes and be motivated to ask, to ask herself actually, "Who will judge the judge?" Recall equally the woman's driving need to separate fact from fiction and be responsible for establishing the truth and making it public when required to do so.

I am on record as condoning the avenging a father's murder in the ancient world so it would be inconsistent of me not to condone avenging a father's murder in the modern world. As I advocated for Orestes in the Athenian court that Aeschylus reported on, I now advocate for Forrest Troyes in the court being assembled in the subconscious mind of Lucy Hunter. Exposé, bringing Forrest to justice, was that the nub of her uncertainty? Apparently so.

As in the dream from the previous night, Lucy participated in a chorus resembling the collective citizenry in a Greek tragedy; this Morpheus concocted chorus, like that in the *Eumenides*, was tuned to the hysterical wailings and complaints of would-be Furies. The dreamscape was ideal for plein-air painting in the impressionist style, very Areopagus in its composition. The dreaming Lucy emerged out of the group as the voice of the prosecution, accusing Forrest Troyes of the unspeakable act of matricide, punishable in full to the letter of the law. She also represented all the guests that bore witness to the dire events on the *Iphigenia* that precipitated the present session in this imagined court of law unfolding in her brain by means of thaumatological manipulation— Vanessa De La Croix, Geoff Canter, Frank Veridis, Inspector Visser, and Captain Vander Valk to mention only the foremost among them, at least those that Lucy had the most accurate recollection of. She addressed these as though they were members of the jury. In the expansive light of the dreamscape,

Morpheus appeared in the guise of Lucy's fellow passenger, Doppelgänger Bert, sitting two seats over, counsel for the defence.

Before proceeding to the arguments forwarded by Lucy's oneiric identity, imperative it was to consider the nature of malfeasance no matter its degree of lethal ruthlessness. Context: the maintenance of civil order and the administration of justice. What followed might have seemed paradoxical but take my word for it as the god of truth and light, there was no contradiction. Of course, self-appointed nit-pickers would likely argue that what I proposed was definitely moot.

A primary function of mine is and always was to make mortals aware of their guilt and having done so, purify them, if they stand accused of offense against the gods or of actions contrary to divine dictate or lawful decrees or codes of law. Understood absolutely! In addition, what should never be overlooked in all of this is the role played by Nemesis, goddess of retribution.

Given that my cursing of Cassandra exemplified what a vengeful god, like an autocratic tyrant, could accomplish to take down a perceived enemy, it was incumbent upon me as covert defence council for Forrest Troyes to amplify the data bank (as it were) of reasonable doubt by providing additional samples of *my* malfeasance. It bespoke action of mine that mirrored the human inclination to exact revenge, for instance, in the manner of Forrest Troyes and, long before him, Orestes.

Asclepius, a son of mine known for his healing powers and the author of numerous medical remedies, was taken down by thunderbolts the Cyclopes fashioned for Zeus, who, by the way, was himself guilty of patricide. I took my revenge for the death of Asclepius by eliminating the Cyclopes, all of them, and ultimately and fortunately avoided reprisals from Zeus. As to King Midas and his just desserts, he should not have declared a preference for Pan's music over mine. I got back at him by turning his ears into those of a donkey. It was intended as more of a joke than anything touching on grim reprisal, but from what I gathered afterward, he and his court laughed very little.

Take the case of Odysseus vis à vis the Sirens and how he succeeded in spiting them. Apparently, he had an ear for music. I inspired these enchantresses to deliver beautiful, enthralling melodies; my intentions were absolutely pure. Odysseus, renowned conniver, was written up in their bad books from way back, from well before the start of the Trojan War. The thing is, I personally had nothing against the great hero although other divinities did. Today Odysseus would likely be into experimental jazz. I mention Poseidon's reprisal against him as an addendum to my theme of not antagonizing the gods or else.

I could go on with additional examples, but I refrain. The point is this: when dealing with Forrest, I understood absolutely the impulse to strike back, to crave revenge for wrongs committed against him, to want to destroy those who destroyed his father and, having done so, rendered his life miserable in just about every sense imaginable.

At this juncture, therefore, let the curtains be drawn open on Lucy Hunter's slumberous reverie as she wings her way over the Grand Banks off Newfoundland. Her courtroom drama, so to say, developed like a debate, counterargument following argument and so on, as would be natural with someone trying to decide between two opposing but equally attractive options.

"Forrest Troyes is charged with conspiracy to commit murder," choral Lucy declared in her opening statement. "In addition to a charge of homicide, he stands accused of matricide, the most heinous of crimes. To date, more than two years after the enactment of immoral and unlawful deeds, he has avoided being brought to justice. For too long the truth has been hidden from public scrutiny. For too long has the perpetrator of indictable crimes escaped retribution. The voice of the people, long muted, must be heard and their will, long denied, must be done. These proceedings are about to bring what has been intentionally hidden or purposefully neglected into sharp focus and thereby lead to remediation of what has been lacking in the pursuit of truth."

All that having been said, Doppelgänger Bert came to the fore and repeated "alleged" several times in statements beneficial to the defence. "Innocent until proven guilty."

The prosecution: "Unequivocal information provided by an accomplice will establish culpability. Factual evidence will substantiate guilt. Witness for the prosecution is Alexsis Troyes, sister and confessed co-conspirator."

The defence: "That same factual evidence will substantiate the opposite. Witness for the defence: Isla Troyes, sister. In *Furies to Juries* she described how Orestes found himself trapped in a moral bind and so very much conflicted over choosing between two goods, one legitimate ethical principle clashing with another. A prototypical example of ethical ambivalence. Forrest was equally subject to similar pressures, legal considerations notwithstanding. In her poem *Forrest Lost*, Isla dramatized how her brother was plagued by compulsive urges to avenge his father's murder; correcting unfavourable family circumstances added to the coercive obligation to right the obvious wrongs he and his siblings were forced to endure, an obligation that had become paramount in his life.

The prosecution's counter argument was that poet Isla Troyes was ignorant, that much of what she wrote was dependent on fanciful supposition, tropes, and displaced loyalty.

The defence continued as follows: "I contend that the accused at the time of the alleged crime was not himself. Forrest Troyes was not autonomous in his actions but dominated by a force superior in strength to his ability to resist. That force was the all-encompassing certainty that his father, Victor Troyes, was murdered by his mother in collaboration with Conrad Steele. At the time of her passing she was known as Kat Steele."

The prosecution: "Is the killing of a mother less serious in its consequences than the killing of a father? To think that such is the case amounts to nothing more than a crotchet draped in the rhetoric of pseudo-male ascendance."

The defence: "Be that as it may, Forrest was psychologically stressed in that he felt mandated to seek vengeance. Proof of this troublesome mental condition is extant."

The prosecution: "Nonetheless, the accused must bear personal responsibility for acts taken contrary to both natural and civil law. Righteous indignation at what life has delivered him is no defense for murder and matricide."

The defence: "Forest Troyes was simply fulfilling his destiny, carrying through on what the Fates had arranged for him. He suffered much throughout his life. It seemed as though he were cursed. Normal cognitive processes failed him periodically. He fell victim to madness."

The prosecution: "Madness evidently resulted from guilt. There is no escaping the ineluctable modalities of conscience. All factors point to his being guilty as sin. Furthermore, hubris played a part in his revenge scheme with his thinking that he could personify the meeting out of justice, that he could take on the role of divine adjudicator, exacting deadly punishment for transgression."

The defence: "Forest Troyes was a man not accountable for his actions, violent or otherwise. Irrationality compelled him. *Actus reus*—madness as readable. Material evidence must be considered here. Exhibits of palpable proof that mental derangement overcame him from time to time."

The prosecution: "Forrest's pathetic anxiety articulated in muddled thought was not too muddled for syntax. His muddied profiles not so muddied as to obscure indications of culpability. His Penseroso moments, such as they are, confirm a mind overwrought with self-accusation and indicate his impulsive attempts to do self-harm."

The defence: "Over wrought with remorse, rather. Shadows are no substitute for substance. Self-loathing is not an indictable offence."

The prosecution: "Forrest Troyes' perverse actions arose from a skewed awareness of pathetic fallacy, distorted for sure and based on self-serving, confirmation-biased literature. In other words, the deafmutes had taken control of the mics, the drums and cymbals."

At this juncture in the dream sequence please permit me, Apollo, mastermind of illusion, to describe how I infused Doppelgänger Bert, arguing in defence of Forrest Troyes, with cogent argumentation, the ultimate in apologetic expostulation. I induced him to wade into the ethical position considered by philosophers and psychologists as rational madness. It equates to enthusiasm in pursuit of perceived good and posits incentive to perform as strong as Eros' inflamed love or a state induced in rituals associated with Dionysus. Plato would certainly be on the same page with me on this point. *Compos mentis* is not in question; stimulation from some daimon of unknown origin is. In other words, something extraordinary is experienced by the individual as affecting ordinary cognitive functions. Call it divine inspiration that drives a mortal toward attaining what is believed to be right and truthful, what is perceived to be *the good.*

My doing, no doubt about it, where Forrest Troyes was concerned. Afflatus trumped culpability.

I also had Doppelgänger Bert introduce into his arguments the Socratic paradox, which concerned affected agency in the service of *the good*, but Lucy did not, surprisingly, pick up on it as an argument to be refuted.

These considerations that Doppelgänger Bert held forth on left Lucy with her dreamy head spinning. She had not in her deliberations considered rational madness as a primary defence in any trial of any description involving Forrest Troyes. Then again, she might have, had she been prompted to do so. Overriding the exculpatory insanity argument proved difficult. Although complete exoneration was out of the question, she conceded the point that Forest Troyes in a state of madness did the "dastardly deeds" and therefore he stood innocent of first degree murder. She agreed on the basis of his being *non-compos mentis* at the time of the murders. When Doppelgänger Bert offered to provide a definition so that nothing was left unclear, she became slightly indignant. She was cognizant, she stated emphatically, of what *non compos mentis* meant: in Forrest Troyes' case, he was not of sound mind and lacked the mental ability to comprehend the nature, consequences, and effects of his actions.

The astute reader of this narrative will point out that overlooked or missing in action in Lucy Hunter's dream court was a jury to produce a verdict based on the evidence presented. The fact remains: in addition to playing the parts of both the prosecution and the defence, Lucy Hunter simultaneously assumed the posts of judge and jury. Such multiplicity in the subconscious of the persona is what makes a dream so fascinating, especially one scripted and orchestrated by the god of inspired jurisprudence, me, Apollo, and featuring the mind-bending art of the god of dreams, Morpheus, conjurer supreme in the space-time of the fantastic. Analogously, when the white light of truth enters the prism of mind, Lucy's in this case, it creates a spectrum of composite iterations, a panoply of colourful subjectivity and points of vantage. Thus enlightened, that same astute reader should therefore conclude that the jury was still undecided when it came to what Lucy Hunter would determine as her best course of action.

Well known is the story of my son Orpheus and his musical fate. Love me, love my lyre, love my boy. On the other hand, I could hardly have fathered Asclepius and not in my own right be involved in the healing arts; I could hardly have failed to make every effort to see Forrest Troyes healed of what ailed him. Under my auspices he evaded what otherwise might have been due punishment, at least he did in Lucy Hunter's dream world, the one I delighted in engineering for the benefit of all attentive readers. In the real world of facts and research and pursuit of truth that she inhabited daily, even I could not prophesize with absolute certainty what her next move regarding events on the *Iphigenia* would be despite my having nudged her subliminally in the dream sequence towards what Aeschylus arranged as an aesthetically and morally justifiable dénouement in his *Eumenides*.

In this mildly turbulent flight of fancy, the notion of redemption remained unbroached. Before awakening, Lucy declared emphatically to all assembled in her plein-air court that Forrest Troyes would be redeemed only when he accepted responsibility for his actions. Soteriological details aside, she continued, Forrest's salvation would depend on his involvement in charitable work and philanthropic donations. A fading Doppelgänger Bert agreed with Lucy in suggesting that whatever munificent contributions Forrest might make, the most significant would be to societies for abused children, especially those maltreated by autocratic fathers and indifferent mothers.

At this juncture I thanked Morpheus, his illustrious and godly self once more. He took himself further along the dimly lit cabin, stopped were an attendant appeared to be responding to the needs of a passenger, and disappeared. I was inclined to follow suit, my involvement in this tale overextended and my disappearance, some would argue, long overdue. A moot point.

Chapter 24
Liminal Space

Somewhere over the north Atlantic, awakened by an announcement from the cockpit regarding possible turbulence ahead, Lucy took notice of where she was. Right, flying home from America to take on the next job the Bureau assigned. The conference and her report of it upstaged by the grand distraction of the Troyes Family saga. What a quixotic few days she'd pushed herself through. She felt as if she were sliding into liminal space again, that betwixt and between state of mind, needing to balance a strange kind of dream wonderment and the real-time sensation of flight in an Airbus A 350. Pulling up the portal shade, she looked out to see a vague kind of distant light and then closed it off again. The UK was hours away.

When the young man at the end of her row retook his seat after exiting the mid-cabin WC, Lucy leaned over to engage him.

"I hope you don't mind my asking if you're a barrister. I get the impression you are."

"Go ahead, ask."

"Are you a barrister?"

"No, I am not a barrister. Do you need one? I will, when I get to where I'm going."

"Not at all. I was just wondering. Trying to judge whether I…"

"No problem, lady. These days I'm an undertaker's understudy."

"That's brilliant. In America, then?"

"Yes. At Gotterup Memorial Gardens out on the island. Family business. Right now I'm on my way to see about an inheritance left me by a distant relative in Bournemouth, England."

"Checking on the body, yeah?"

"Checking to see if it's the real deal and not some sort of scam. The jury's still out on that one, as my old man likes to say when in doubt. Anyways, lady—"

"Righto. I just thought to ask. I have no need of a lawyer. You see, you remind me a great deal of a waiter I recently met in Greenwich Village."

"A good looking dude, was he, lady? Now if…"

Lucy got the impression that the young bloke was trying to stay to himself, to keep quiet like the rest of the passengers in the dimly lit cabin. She dropped back in her seat, satisfied that she had at least followed up on a premonition, futile though it proved to be.

"Thanks," she said in a muffled tone.

"No problem."

Like mad Forrest caught in a moral bind, like Orestes equally cursed, Lucy continued in the twilight of her acquiescence to wrestle with determining the right course of action for her once she'd signed off with the Guv at the Bureau. The facts were known, therefore no need to hypothesize about probabilities any longer. So, to reveal the truth or to keep silent about it. That was the question. To say nothing was to undermine her life's work and be deemed complicit, a silent partner in a conspiracy to commit murder, that being an unwelcome defamation in her own mind at least. To keep schtum and leave it all in a grey area where justice and vengeance conflict.

Or.

Or what?

To reveal all and break a promise and betray a trust and in the process destroy lives and consequently be thrust into the vortex of an official inquiry. The carceral implications for Flex, Forrest, and Alexsis were overwhelming and too devastating to entertain in terms of decided action.

Before deplaning at Heathrow, Lucy posed herself a simple, direct question, relevant to all that she'd read and all that she'd put herself through the last three days, to mention nothing of the last few hours. "What would Apollo do?"

Allow me to override point of view one last time. In response to the question Lucy Hunter asked herself, I, Apollo, would pose another. "Cui bono?"

The End

[If you enjoyed this book, please leave your author a review. Reviews are very important to authors because they help readers find books they will enjoy reading.]

[BWL Author name tag for Reed Stirling]

Reed Stirling lives in Cowichan Bay, BC, and writes when not painting landscapes, or travelling, or taking coffee at The Drumroaster, a local café where physics and metaphysics clash daily.

Novels with BWL Publishing:
Shades Of Persephone (2019) is a literary mystery set in Greece.

Lighting The Lamp (2020) is a fictional memoir.

Set in Montreal, *Séjour Saint-Louis (2021),* dramatizes family conflicts.

The Palimpsest Murders (2023) is a European travel mystery set in the Lowlands.

A Bouquet of Darts (2024) features Eros, the mischievous god of love.

Reed Stirling's shorter work has appeared over the years in a variety of publications including *Hackwriters Magazine, Dis(s)ent, The Danforth Review,*

Fickle Muses, The Fieldstone Review, StepAway Magazine, Mediterranean Poetry, and *Humanist Perspectives.*

[BWL Publishing Logo and Canada.ca url]

276